While I wasn't ever snatched from death or dishonor myself, the ghost left her mark on me too. It all happened when I was no longer a child nor yet old enough to be anything else. I was getting long in the leg but was still short on experience. This is always a difficult age to sort out or live through. All I know for sure is that ever after the ghost, I was changed somewhat and possibly wiser.

RICHARD PECK was born in Decatur, Illinois. He attended Oxford University in England and holds degrees from DePauw University and Southern Illinois University. He is the author of *Close Enough to Touch*, *Through a Brief Darkness*, *Representing Super Doll*, *Dreamland Lake*, *Secrets of the Shopping Mall*, *Are You in the House Alone?*, and *Ghosts I Have Been* (a sequel to *The Ghost Belonged to Me*), all available in Dell Laurel-Leaf editions. Mr. Peck lives in New York City.

The Ghost
❧ Belonged to Me ❧

A NOVEL BY

RICHARD PECK

LAUREL-LEAF BOOKS bring together under a single imprint
outstanding works of fiction and nonfiction particularly
suitable for young adult readers, both in and out of the
classroom. Charles F. Reasoner, Professor Emeritus of
Children's Literature and Reading, New York University,
is consultant to this series.

Published by
Dell Publishing Co., Inc.
1 Dag Hammarskjold Plaza
New York, New York 10017

Laurel-Leaf Library ® TM 766734, Dell Publishing Co., Inc.

ISBN: 0-440-93075-8

RL: 5.9

Reprinted by arrangement with The Viking Press
Printed in the United States of America
First Laurel-Leaf printing—August 1983
Second Laurel-Leaf printing—November 1983

This book is dedicated to
DOROTHY BUSH and HELEN BUSH
in friendship

The Ghost
Belonged to Me

❧ 1 ❧

AT ONE TIME THERE WAS A GHOST OUT in the brick barn on the back of our place.

There are several opinions that people hold regarding ghosts, and not one of them would clinch an argument. Some people will swallow the idea of ghosts in general but draw the line at any one ghost in particular. And there are people who will take to ghosts because they're naturally morbid. Or because they're in touch with earlier times, like my great-uncle, Miles Armsworth. Then there are some who claim they are reserving judgment on the entire subject until science has its say.

Since I'm having my say now, I tell you we had a ghost and she haunted our barnloft. It was a girl ghost, and while unnerving, not hideous. And though she was not particularly welcome, she made herself very useful in the weird ways that ghosts operate. You probably wonder why a girl dead many years would take an interest in the activities of living strangers. But as I found out, ghosts have feelings too, and if they are not human, at least they once were.

In a way, the ghost belonged to me. But she was a secret I could not keep, and so other people were drawn in. A boy is hard to believe, as the ghost herself once said. But whether they believed me or not, a number of people would have met a terrible end but for her intervention and mine.

And when you come to consider it from all angles, the ghost even saved my sister Lucille from a fate worse than death. Today, she's Mrs. Lowell Seaforth, one of the most respected young women in town, ask anybody.

While I wasn't ever snatched from death or dishonor myself, the ghost left her mark on me too. It all happened when I was no longer a child nor yet old enough to be anything else. I was getting long in the leg but was still short on experience. This is always a difficult age to sort out or live through. All I know for sure is that ever after the ghost, I was changed somewhat and possibly wiser.

The whole story of this business starts a good while back, as stories will. It was a time when people were still talking about the marvels of the Louisiana Purchase Exposition World's Fair of 1904 held down at St. Louis. At least my mother's cousin, Mrs. Elvera Schumate, talked at length about it. She'd come to money sooner than the rest of us due to marrying the late Mr. Schumate. And where she wanted to go, she went.

Visiting the World's Fair gave her a lifetime of contemplation on mankind's diversity, as she often says. There's hardly a topic you can raise without reminding Cousin Elvera of a point of interest down at the fair.

Because of the ghost, I happened to venture out into the world a good deal farther than St. Louis. But this hasn't stilled Cousin Elvera's voice on the subject of her own experiences which she gladly relates to anybody who'll listen.

"Attend my words, Alexander," she'll say, grabbing hold of my arm, "the world outside Bluff City is full of mysteries and wonders undreamed of in your limited experience." There have also been some mysteries and wonders closer to home that confounded even Cousin Elvera, though I don't know as she gives them much thought anymore.

Back at the time of the ghost, electrified street cars were beginning to give Bluff City an up-to-date appearance. They hooked up with the interurban network and you could even cross the Mississippi River at various points. People said that if you kept switching from car to car you could travel all the way to New York City or Denver, whichever place you wanted to go to.

My dad's uncle, Miles Armsworth, who was a roamer, once rode clear to Wheeling, West Virginia, on the interurban in three days and a night. It took him five days back, though, and he said that was because he'd been misdirected and rode a day in the wrong direction. My mother said it was because he drank.

There are trolleys passing day and night behind our barn. They go on to cross the trestle over Snake Creek near the end of the line. In seasonable weather, they run the open-sided cars, and you can hear the people talking as they glide behind the barn.

You'd think that kind of continual buzz and clatter would send a ghost off looking for a more deathly type place to haunt. But it didn't.

William Howard Taft of Cincinnati had just finished up being president of the United States. It was 1913, and I was turning thirteen years old. That's the time I'm telling you about.

There was a spunky streak in me that led to occasional trouble, nothing serious. It didn't bother anybody much except my teacher, Miss Winkler, who by her own admission strives for "the habit of perfection."

She and I have had our run-ins, but I won't call the roll of them since they don't bear on this story. In fact, Miss Winkler was one of the last holdouts when it came to facing up to the actual existence of ghosts.

She'd have been a lot more pleased with the both of us if she could have gotten me to knuckle down and apply myself to scholarship. "You could be one of the sharpest tacks in the carpet if you would only find your-self a direction, Alexander," she'd say. But she never leaned on me to her full capacity for fear of locking horns with my mother.

She did call in my dad one time for a private word.

As much as I got out of him later was that she said though I had "the gift of a glib tongue," I lacked the moral sense for preaching or leadership. And as my father, he'd be doing his duty if he aimed me toward a useful trade.

Since my dad prefers useful trades himself to the line of work he's in now, he agreed with her. So I went every Saturday for a while to The Apex Automotive Garage to learn the mechanic's trade, which is the coming thing.

Apex had converted from a livery stable when people started switching over to automobiles. A friend of mine, name of Bub Timmons, was learning the trade there too, so I enjoyed the work.

There isn't any knowing where this might have led except one day old man Leverett brought in his Haynes-Apperson with the brake band spewing out fabric and copper wire. He'd bought that Haynes-Apperson used in 1907, so it was past its prime anyway. It was one of those old-timey models with a whipsocket.

Bub and I went to work and stripped the wheel down and commenced repacking it. But we ran short of brake lining and filled in with what we could find.

The outcome of this was that on his way home old man Leverett set his brakes at the level crossing on the Ocean-to-Ocean Highway west of town. The brakes gave out on him, and the auto nosed up on the track just as the Wabash Railroad's *City of Joliet* came high-balling through.

The locomotive caught it just behind the headlamps, and you could pick up Haynes-Apperson parts anywhere along the embankment for a mile. They found the front left wheel, and that led them to discover it was half packed with cotton wadding. And they found old man Leverett face up in the ditch already saying he'd take his mechanical business elsewhere and have a word with his friends too. So that was the end of my apprenticeship. Apex kept Bub Timmons on for some reason, though I don't begrudge him a trade. He needs the work. But I was kind of at loose ends after my mechanical learning came to nothing. The next thing I was to learn about was girls.

If it had been left up to me, I wouldn't have started with Blossom Culp. It was her who started with me. Blossom and her folks live behind our place on the far side of the car tracks just about on a straight line with our barn. There's a row of houses back there that people move in and out of. The row was built for the workers at the flour mill until they wouldn't live there anymore. I didn't know anything about the Culps at that time and had been looking straight through Blossom for two grades. I couldn't even tell you when they first drifted into town.

Oh, one time back around fifth grade Blossom offered to let me wear her spelling medals if I'd walk her home from school, but I wasn't falling for that. She's an exceptional speller, which always seems to surprise Miss Winkler.

Blossom has big round button eyes, very dark and sharp, and wears black wool stockings right through the school year. Her legs are the skinniest I've seen. When my sister Lucille came to notice Blossom, she labeled her an "arachnid," which is what they call spiders in the high-school biology class. That was a rude observation, but it's true that Blossom does have a spidery look.

I fell into her web during a fire drill at school. We have them once a month by law. I go to the Horace Mann School, which is a strictly modern structure. They have it fitted out with the last word in fire escapes.

It's a long sheet-metal tube that angles out of the second-floor cloakroom and down to a sandpile beside the foundation. It's better than a playground slide because it echoes.

The bell went one day in early May, and we all let rip with a whoop. Miss Winkler twitched and said, "We'll have order here. This may be the real thing!" She says that once a month.

Blossom was just ahead of me when we trooped to the cloakroom, which I know now was not by chance. Miss Winkler threw open the little doors down by the baseboard. Then she spaced us as we went down, saying to every kid in turn, "Don't yell and light running."

It's my private opinion that in a real fire the tube would heat up like a stove flue, and I'd sooner take my chances on the stairs.

Blossom flopped down and shot away. Miss Winkler had me by the arm to the count of three. Then she turned me loose, and down I went. You start slow and gather speed. From the top, the daylight at the bottom looks no bigger than a bright dime.

That day I was skidding on my hands to enjoy a slower ride when I glanced down between my feet and saw the tube was all clogged up halfway along. It's as dark as a pocket in that thing, but I knew it had to be Blossom Culp who was wedged sideways. Her petticoats were over her head. Both legs were up against the top, and she was clinging onto a welded seam with all her fingers. She came near to turning herself inside out, and I knew as soon as I saw her she'd jammed herself on purpose.

I had all I could do to keep from hitting her square on with my hobnail boots. That would have marked her for life, so I went into a spin myself. And there we were, packed in at an angle and somebody up at the top waiting to start down.

When I hit Blossom, I was all over her. I had my hands where I'd never handled a girl before, but my mind wasn't on it.

"Blossom," I said, "you don't know if you're coming or going. Turn loose of that seam, or we'll be backed up all the way to Winkler."

"Listen to me," she said with her lips right up against my ear. "I have vital information for you alone. It has to do with forces that only you can comprehend."

"What is this?" I said. "Will you give way? This tube wasn't built for a crowd."

"Promise!" Blossom breathed at me. "Promise you'll walk me home from school because I have news of special benefit to you."

"Blossom—"

"Promise, or I'll set to screaming."

I promised Blossom. What else could I do, halfway across her with my head upside down and Miss Winkler hollering down the tube? Blossom went limp then, and down we skidded cheek by jowl and heads first. Just as we came to the dip at the end, Blossom reached out and grabbed me around the neck. And that's the way we spilled out onto the sand pile, right at the feet of the principal, Miss Mae Spaulding.

I tried to roll free but went the wrong way and did a turn right over Blossom, who then drew up her knees and did a quick kind of back flip and stood up like an acrobat. "Well, I've seen everything now," said Miss Spaulding. "Cut and run, you two." We did but not before I saw a grin spread across Miss Spaulding's face that I don't think I ever will get over.

I could've boxed Blossom's ears for that, but I walked her home that night instead. I didn't owe her anything, and I didn't think she had any secrets to impart. But I walked her home.

❧ 2 ❧

I TOLD BLOSSOM TO MEET ME TWO corners away from the school. A promise is a promise, but I wasn't having anybody see me walk out of the schoolyard with a girl, any girl.

As it turned out, our meeting place was right outside Nirider's Notions store that does a penny candy business. Blossom was looking hard at Nirider's window. But I walked right on by, brushing against her so she'd notice I was there, keeping my promise.

She caught up with me and hit my stride. I walked along with my head down, watching her petticoats switching along over her black spider legs and noticing there were buttons off her shoes. We walked as far as the Baptist Chapel without a word passed. But I could listen in on Blossom's mind, gauging how far we were to home and getting ready to tell me some nonsense or other.

"If you walk this fast, we'll be home before you learn what I have to tell you," she said.

"This here is my regular pace," I told her.

"Well, slow it in your own best interests," she said.

How I had come to be nagged by Blossom Culp was uppermost in my mind. I slowed down.

"My mama was born with a caul," she said, starting thoughtful and quiet. "You know cauls?"

"Maybe."

"A caul is a mystical veil over the face, like a damp sheet but transparent, and them born with it are born to second sight. Their eyes see through the darkness that blinds others."

"Cats see in the dark," I offered. "And they don't know you can't. You can tread on a cat in the dark before he knows to move out of your path."

"Not that kind of dark," Blossom said, very patient. "The kind of dark that clouds mankind's mind. Dark of the spirit. My mama sees the Unseen."

I was beginning to remember something about Blossom Culp I hadn't thought of for maybe a couple of years. When she first came to town, she let it be known around the school that at birth she'd been one-half of a pair of Siamese twins.

To hear her tell it, they'd had to hack off the twin stuck on her side in order for her alone to live. A bunch of fourth-grade girls got fed up hearing this tale and set on her in the girls' washroom one time. They jerked her shirtwaist up and her skirt down to see if they could see the scar from where her twin had been taken off. But she was just as smooth-sided as anybody. From then on none of the girls would have anything to do with her.

"The Gift's in the family," Blossom said, "but I don't have it. Neither does my paw. Oh, he used to could cure warts by passing his hand over the affected area, but he don't do anything regular. There's gypsy blood in the family, Mama's side. She had a sister who foretold the San Francisco earthquake—saw buildings falling and fire raging four days ahead of time. When she heard her prophecy was become manifest, she frothed at the mouth, and we had to lay a spoon across her tongue to keep it from going down her windpipe. We're from Sikeston. That's in Missouri. You know Sikeston?"

"Maybe."

"It's a place neither North nor South. Farthest up-river cotton grows. It blows like snow across the road at picking time. Sikeston's a wonderful place for the Unseen. Ghosts of both the Confederate and Union forces, wandering, wandering, forever wandering, trying to get to a Christian grave. My mama has saw them going by the house many a time, with their canteens swinging and dragging their rifles. A ghost battalion. Made her heart bleed, she said."

I wasn't rising up to any such bait as that. I just kept trudging and picking at the foliage in the hedges to show Blossom my whole attention wasn't on her.

"It was quiet for Mama when we moved up here," she went on, "until she seen the halo from the sink.

"Mama sees halos sometimes, in colors. And they

16

only mean but one thing. A sure sign—and Mama seen one when she was standing at the sink, looking out the window at the back of you folks's barn."

"If there's a halo round our barn, I reckon it fell off a passing angel. He'll very likely be back to pick it up when he misses it."

"You don't want to talk light of halos," Blossom said. "They're a sure sign."

"What of?"

"They're a sign that a place is haunted. The halo tells it and the color tells who."

"What who?"

"The kind of ghost that's haunting it. The halo round your barn is pale pink. That means it's the ghost of a young girl, cut off in her prime or sooner."

"Sunsets turn things pink. Especially brick."

"Sun sets in the other direction. Anyhow, Mama sees it at night. Late."

"You ever see it?"

"No, I don't see nothing. I ain't got the Gift. Mama says the Gift is running thin, and when she's gone we'll be just like other people. Common. I don't do much too well except spell, and that don't mean anything to Mama. Someday I'm just going to light out on my own."

Now that took me by surprise. I thought sure Blossom was going to claim she could see what wasn't there to make herself interesting. And here she was saying she didn't have the Gift. Not that I fell for that Gift business anyway.

"Your mama seen the ghost itself or only this pink halo?"

"Oh, Mama don't approach a ghost. But she knows." We were walking past a horse trough full of green water about then. And I had an urge to give Blossom a big shove right in it to cool off her storytelling. But the way she was going on, I had an idea she'd just settle into the trough and keep right on talking in that soft and steady way of hers.

"How come you're telling me all this?"

"Mama says you're receptive. Maybe you have the Gift and maybe not. But she says you're receptive. You can make contact with the Unseen if you take a notion to, that's what Mama says."

"Your mama doesn't even know me."

"Mama don't need the Gift to know you. We live right behind you. Maybe you don't see us, but we see you."

"Maybe I'll have a word with your mama about this. How'd you like that?" I thought I was calling her bluff the same as those girls did the time they looked to see if she was one half of Siamese twins. But Blossom just said, "You can try it if you want to, but Mama don't tell anything without you paying her. And if you pay her, she'll say anything that comes into her head. But you can try if you want to."

That didn't make a believer out of me, but it had me stumped. Just when I thought I'd catch Blossom, her words would ooze away.

Before we got to the Pine Street intersection, our house came into view. It's the third biggest house in town, with a good deal of brickwork and carpentry to it. It was built back in the days when people put a lot of style into everything. There's three-quarters of an acre of yard which we've got a bronze deer in and three big flower beds bordered in shells. And there's a porch roof thrown out from one side that you can drive a team through and let off callers dry-shod in case of rain. Of course, we have an automobile now. And in spite of what Blossom was saying, I thought it was the only thing we had in the barn.

Our house is a regular showplace, though my dad says he could have had a new, strictly modern house built with twice the convenience at half the price. But buying the third biggest house in town was my mother's idea. Blossom glanced up at it and knew time was running out.

I walked her up our lane, though, and back past the barn. But I never let her notice when I glanced up at the barn to see if there might be something extra showing. With my imagination somewhat inflamed, I could picture a big rainbow-looking thing arching up over the lightning rods. Blossom talks a good line, and I'll give her that.

I figured I'd walk her as far as the tracks. Then she could hoof it from there by herself. An open streetcar went past and made a stop down at the corner.

My sister Lucille was climbing down out of the car,

but luckily she didn't notice me seeing Blossom home. Lucille took the streetcar home from the high school because she wouldn't walk eight blocks under any circumstances, unless maybe it was on the arm of Tom Hackett. She was carrying her book satchel and a hatbox from the Select Dry Goods Company, Lucille not being able to walk past a store without going in and buying something.

She was wearing one of those stiff straw hats girls were beginning to wear then, like men's hats only bigger in the brim. "That's my sister Lucille," I remarked to Blossom for something to say.

"I know it," Blossom replied. "She's a dressy kind of girl."

"She goes out with Tom Hackett," I mentioned.

"I know it," Blossom replied. "She'll marry him if she gets half a chance."

How these Culps came by all their information beat the devil out of me. "She'd better make haste, though," Blossom went on, "because these big, full-figured girls are beginning to go out of style, and Tom Hackett'll turn his attentions elsewhere."

I looked at Lucille in the distance, bobbing over the track and sashaying up across the back lawn to the house. She was a pretty substantial figure at that, and I'd never noticed. "She's dressy, though," Blossom repeated.

My mother called the way she and Lucille dressed "elegant." I informed Blossom of that. "No," she said.

"Not elegant—dressy." And then she stepped over the car tracks in her busted shoes and her snagged black stockings and her patched skirt. I watched her all the way to her back porch, which had a washtub hung up by the door. Then I turned around and faced the barn.

❦ 3 ❧

THERE WERE COBWEBS ALL OVER THE
steps up to what used to be the haymow. Really rich
people like the Van Deeters and the Breckenridges and
the Hacketts make their servants live up in their lofts
now that they don't need the fodder space. But we just
closed ours off for storage since we don't have any
live-in help.

I went from Blossom to the barn just to have a look
around and see if our automobile was okay. Inside,
everything looked regular, and I was thinking seriously
about checking around upstairs, though I could see from
the cobwebs that nobody had been up there in quite
some time.

Our automobile is a Mercer, and it's so big that we
had to tear out the loose boxes and the tack room and
all the barn fittings to give it room. Riches haven't
bought a whole lot that my dad puts much value on, except for the Mercer.

It stood there with its oil cups brimming and its brightwork gleaming. "Money wouldn't buy a better machine," my dad says, and, "They'll never build them any better."

It's a C model, with fifty-eight horsepower. The best day my dad ever lived was when he drove it back from the factory at Milwaukee, Wisconsin, and wheeled into the Bluff City Square. There were faces at every window of the Abraham Lincoln Hotel Billiard Parlor. People well acquainted with my dad knew he had laid out twenty-six hundred dollars cash money for it. And those who knew told those who didn't.

He'd bought it from the Beaver Manufacturing Company at Milwaukee and personally shook the hand of the designer—Finlay Robertson Porter, "a gentleman but down-to-earth" was how he struck Dad.

The Mercer is enameled bright yellow, like all Mercers, with air-dried rock-maple chassis and axles. The accelerator's out on the runningboard.

I was three steps up the barnloft stairs slowing down to watch a dusty sunbeam just catch the brass fittings on the Mercer's headlamps. That was when I heard the whimpering.

A little crying whine. Then nothing. Then the little whine again and a scratching. A hornet buzzed down from a nest he'd built in against a ceiling beam. I didn't want that sound to be coming from upstairs. It could have been a starling. They get in upstairs. They can get in places, and you can't figure how. But they don't whine.

I thought about heading on back up to the house. But I knew the minute I hit outdoors, I'd break into a run. And I didn't want Blossom Culp to see that, if she was watching from wherever she watches.

The hinge on the upstairs door wanted oil. I reached up and pushed it open. If a starling flew out, I didn't want to jump and maybe lose my footing.

Nothing came out but a beam of low afternoon sunlight. It's brighter upstairs because of the big window with colored-glass borders to match the house.

While I stood on the steps listening for more sounds, the elastic garter on my right leg gave out and unwound. It took my sock with it slow and easy from right in under my knicker leg down to a heap around my shoetop. But I never moved until I heard a sniffy kind of sob. It sounded like it came from under water.

I was pretty nearly blinded by that sun coming in level. But I took some comfort from the light. So I mounted one more step. That put my eye even with the crack in the door. I saw a jumble of low shapes through it—bowed-top trunks probably. Sticking up out of them was a shape, bright where the sun hit it, dark behind. It was a woman's shape, and no question about it. But nothing whatever about the shoulders—like the Headless Horseman.

Then I heard growling, way back in a throat. A wet finger of sweat started down the back of my neck. I burst up the last step and banged the door back. Before I got stopped, I was just about in the middle of the room with dust fogging up all around. I whirled and looked my mother's old dress form square in the busts. They were big, round, and solid, looking very much like my mother did a few years back. I felt like a big relieved fool.

Then I heard the sound right at my feet. I looked down at a mess of matted fur. It was a scrawny little lap dog looking up at me with eyes that recalled Blossom Culp's, but filmy. And how it came to be hunkered down at my feet all of the sudden I didn't know.

Somewhat perplexed, I reached down to pick her up. She took a little halfhearted nip at my hand, and when I worked in under her belly she let out a cry. Then she scrambled up on three legs, favoring a front paw, and tried to limp across the floor with the one paw drawn up.

She was dragging a pink ribbon somebody had tied around her neck. The ribbon was in tatters and looked well chewed.

When she peeped back at me with her little pushed-in face, I knew she wanted to be friendly. So I scooped her up and felt she was wringing wet. There were puddles around on the floor too. Which is natural if a dog's been shut in. The place smelled bad, but not like dog mess. It was a musty smell of damp, though there's a good slate roof on the barn.

I never entertained the notion of taking the dog to

the house. The minute my mother saw it, she'd call the pound. She grew up on a tenant farm surrounded by many a four-legged critter, but she's put all that behind her now.

When the dog finally let me, I handled her front paw enough to know it was fractured. So I nipped down the stairs to find a couple of laths I could skin off an orange crate and whittle down for splints. I was much encouraged to have ghosts off my mind. And already planning to keep that dog up in the loft, feed her regular, and make her my own. She was an indoor dog anyway and wouldn't mind the confinement. She'd belonged to somebody, so like as not she was paper-trained.

Later, when I had her bound up with splints and tire patches, I made a bed for her out of the remains of the crate and an old shawl. I brought her a coffee can of water from the downstairs tap and planned on slipping her some food. When I left the loft, her big eyes followed me to the door.

It was pretty near evening then, and I'd have some questions to answer when I got up to the house. But when I'd pulled the barn doors to behind me, I lingered a while. There was an old stone hitching post by the drive. It was left from horse days, sunk in the time of Captain Campbell who built the place.

The top of the post is carved like a pony's mouth coming up out of acanthus leaves with an iron ring in its mouth. Down at the base in tall grass were initials cut into a panel: I. D. I'd seen those letters so often that I didn't wonder what they signified.

I fiddled with the hitch ring and contemplated Blossom Culp. She was brazen enough to plant a small dog up in the barn just to give some weight to her storytelling. She was brazen enough for anything. But she was a liar, I decided, and from a long line of them.

I planned to slip back after supper with food and a curry comb to get some of the mud out of the dog's tangles, which I did. I figured once she got her food from me, she'd be mine. When I went back later, she wouldn't eat, but she looked grateful. I named her Trixie.

I was in bed that night after my second trip to the barn, grinning in the dark about Blossom Culp and pink halos. If there was such a thing as a ghost, I figured it would haunt the house, not the barn. And it wouldn't be any young girl cut off in her prime.

It'd be old Captain Campbell, who built this place and hanged himself in it before the mortar was dry. Nobody remembered just which of the twenty-three rooms it was where he'd strung himself up. Ever since I was quite a small kid, I had roamed through the rooms, wondering which one it was.

Very nearly all the downstairs rooms have eighteen-foot ceilings, which would have put the captain to a lot of trouble with a tall ladder and a long rope. The word was that Captain Campbell did himself in before he got well acquainted. Nobody seemed to know how he came by his money. Some said he'd been a captain in the Civil War. Which didn't explain the fortune he'd put into the house he hadn't hardly finished before he did away with himself.

Mother wouldn't hear any talk on the subject. And I never thought for a minute she'd allow a ghost in the house. Certain people thought we got the place cheap since it had an evil name from standing empty all those years. But my dad said that any place that cost fifty-five dollars a winter to heat was not his idea of a bargain.

On account of all this deep thinking, I didn't drop right off to sleep. I twisted around in the bed till my nightshirt was in a knot up under my neck. Which only made me think stronger about old Captain Campbell.

It's possible that I drifted off for a minute, but no longer. The ironwork on the ceiling fixture threw a pattern across the room. There was a light breeze ballooning the curtains. I got up to close the window.

It faces the barn. I looked maybe a whole minute in that direction before I owned up to what I was seeing. It was a moonless night, and there's a Dutch elm tree to throw more shadow.

The dormer window on the barn was candlelit. The colored glass border panes were awash with light. And there was candle flame at the window, haloed with fuzzy yellow. Pinkish-yellow.

The breeze whipped up my nightshirt, and my heart hammered my ribs. Then I made a run for the bed. I grabbed up my pillow and took off down the hall to a spare bedroom facing the front of the house. In there is a high brass bed with an extra comforter folded at the foot. I shot the bolt behind me. Just as I was climbing into the bed, I heard voices drifting up. The window in that room looks down on the open part of the porch.

They were human voices, and I knew whose they were. I crept over to the window to listen a while.

Down on what Mother calls the piazza Lucille was entertaining Tom Hackett on a bentwood settee. I couldn't see them clear, but then I didn't need to.

"Oh, Tom," says Lucille, "you better never do *that!*"

"Come on, Lucille, you know you want—"

"I know I want you to mind your manners, Tom Hackett!"

"I won't mind if you don't mind."

"Oh, Tom. Oh . . ."

Oh good grief, is what I thought. I crept back to bed and began drifting off right away. Before I slept, though, I had a picture of Blossom creeping up the loft steps in the middle of the night to light a candle that could burn the whole durn place down. Then I had a picture of Blossom sound asleep in her bed, untroubled by a guilty conscience. Then I slept, but I tossed some.

❦ 4 ❧

I ROSE UP NEXT MORNING OUT OF THE wrong bed, sure that Blossom's scheming was at the bottom of everything. While I waited ten hours for Lucille to get out of the bathroom, I worked my brains as to how I could square myself with Blossom. The usual earthworms and slimy slugs in the lunchpail wouldn't faze her. I cast about for something that would.

I was still casting at the breakfast table, where I'd finally gone direct because I never did get into the bathroom.

"Alexander, those ears don't look scrubbed to me," Mother observed. My face was low in a plate of breaded pork chops, cottage fries, and eggs that Gladys had just put in front of me.

She saved the day by saying to Mother, "If Lucille ain't comin' down, Mrs. Armsworth, I'm not wrastlin' a tray up to her room."

I couldn't see Dad for the newspaper up over his face. He had it folded lengthwise and was drinking coffee on the other side of it. I could tell how his high collar was grabbing at his throat from the sound of gulping when he swallowed.

Right about then, Lucille charged into the dining room, looking a little baggy-eyed. "I'm here," she sang out to the kitchen door.

And from the other side Gladys yelled, "You better be."

"Hello, Brother dear," Lucille said to me and whipped up all the hair on my head as she slid her sizable bottom into a chair.

"Lemme alone," I greeted her.

"Lucille," Mother said, working her rings, "when *will* you stop hollering from room to room at the servant?"

The servant came through the door with Lucille's chops and eggs and wished out loud that certain people would refer to her as the hired girl instead of a servant because out in the country where we *all of us* originated, hired help wasn't called servants.

Mother let that pass but set on Lucille again. "I fell into a fitful sleep last night before I heard the front door lock behind you and on a school night too. If Tom Hackett can't see you home at a reasonable hour, I'm very much afraid there are going to have to be some rules set down." She looked toward the folded newspaper, "by your father." Dad is deaf when he gets be-hind his newspaper, which in this instance could have meant agreement.

"I guess if Tom Hackett isn't doing right, you'd rather see me stepping out with—ah—Bub Timmons," Lucille said, very pert.

"Don't talk so absurd," Mother said. "Bub Timmons is no more than fourteen years old.

"And trash," Lucille added.

At the mention of Bub, Dad glanced around his news-paper, trying to decipher how the Timmonses had come into the conversation. But he ducked back when Lucille continued. "What if I was to break it off with Tom?" Lucille said to Mother. "Then how'd you feel? You been grooming me for Tom and the Hackett money since I was younger than this squirt here." Lucille waved a knife in my direction.

"Don't talk so vulgar," Mother said, glancing over her shoulder at the kitchen door. "And put down your knife when you're using your fork."

I heard a horse stomping gravel and glanced behind me out the bay window. There was Uncle Miles Arms-worth, eighty-five years old and straight as a plumb line. He was tying his horse, Nelly Melba, up to the porch post. His big box of carpentry tools was fixed onto the back of his buggy. So I knew we were in for an inter-ruption before Lucille and Mother could get each other by the short hairs.

Pretty soon the front door banged back, and Uncle Miles bellowed down the hall, "ANYBODY TO HOME?"

"Oh dear Lord, not this early," Mother sighed and rubbed her forehead.

"I better be off to school," said Lucille.

"Fold your napkin," Mother told her.

"Come on in, Uncle Miles!" Dad said, turning so he wouldn't have to look at Mother.

Lucille was beating a hasty retreat, but she said to Mother, "Be sure to tell Uncle Miles what we want him to build for my party."

"First things first," Mother said. "I want him to get started on the porch today. You know how difficult he is."

Then Uncle Miles was standing in the doorway grinning toothless like he just tagged us all out in a turn at hide-and-seek.

"Still settin' to your breakfast!" he boomed. "I had mine at 5:30!"

Uncle Miles was an original kind of old codger and a sore trial to Mother. Dad would have put him on the payroll at the business, which is house construction. But Uncle Miles was an independent type carpenter. He took on the work he wanted to and worked a ten-hour day. Then he'd lay off for a week to fish Snake Creek or travel. Taking so many odd jobs all over town kept him modern, he always said.

Cousin Elvera Schumate said his way with wood

was as admired as his tongue was feared. She would say this much on his behalf even if she is from Mother's side of the family.

"Come on in, Uncle Miles, and take a—" Dad caught a glimpse of Mother before he could ask him to sit down. But Gladys slammed through from the kitchen and advanced on him with a beaming face and a cup of coffee.

"Say, Gladys, if I'd a-knowed I'd see you, I'd a-put my teeth in." Uncle Miles fumbled around in his overall pocket and pulled out a full set of false choppers. They grinned out of his fist at Gladys, who whooped a big laugh. Mother shaded her eyes with her hand.

"That will do, Gladys," she moaned.

"Oh hark at that, Gladys?" said Uncle Miles. "Back to the kitchen while you're still an honest woman. But stay single for me. I'm just a-gettin' into my prime!" Gladys whooped again and vanished.

"Well, Uncle Miles, how you feeling?" Dad said.

"Better'n you look, Joe. You gettin' to look more and more like a pinch-faced banker right along. Settin' at a desk when you'd be better workin' construction in the great out-of-doors. Ain't you laid up enough money yet to suit—"

"Uncle Miles!" Mother said, half out of her chair and her mind, "I want you to remove some of the scrollwork from off the front porch and start thinking about a balustrade for the piazza."

"For the pi—what, Luella?" Uncle Miles turned his spectacles on Mother in surprise.

"For the *piazza*, Uncle Miles. But first I want you to saw off some of those geegaws and gimcracks from the porch entrance. All of that jigsaw ornamentation is passing out of fashion."

"Hark at who's tellin' who what's passin' out of fashion," Uncle Miles said to the ceiling. "You better get a plasterer in here, Luella. Your wall's crackin' above the plate rail."

Mother glanced up toward the ceiling without meaning to. "Never mind that, Uncle Miles. What I want you to do is—"

"To rebuild this here house that old Captain Campbell built in eighteen-hunnert and sixty-one to last a thousand years. And you want it rebuilt this morning with a key-hole saw, that about it?"

"All I want," Mother tried to explain, "is—"

"Course without the gingerbread, this house is goin' to look pretty near naked. It was meant to have steamboat trim and without it, the place'll look a lot like a grain elevator."

Dad snorted.

"Don't you start, Joe," Uncle Miles said with a twinkle sparkling in his eye. "Your company knocks together four overpriced houses a week for poor saps as will pay three thousand dollars for 'em, but I don't notice you livin' in one." He turned suddenly on Mother. "How about Grecian columns to support the porch roof, Luella?"

"Why—"

"Hacketts have Grecian columns on their porch."

"Do they?" Mother said. "I hadn't noticed."

"You would if you was invited there. But then the Hacketts has a lot of things other folks don't." Since Uncle Miles hadn't been asked to sit, he kept walking around the dining-room table holding his coffee cup very dainty. A big ball-peen hammer was swinging on his hip.

"Of course, I knowed the Hacketts when," he said, circling around behind my chair.

"When?" I asked him.

"Why hello there, Alexander!" he boomed right into my ear. "Why I knowed the Hacketts when they was workin' out of a single drug store in an alley off the square. Not even a paved alley. They was rollin' their patent medicine pills one at a time when I knowed 'em. But now ain't they high and mighty and already goin' to seed! And all because of their big factory turnin' out—"

"Pharmaceuticals," Mother said in desperation.

"Laxatives!" Uncle Miles said in triumph.

"Got the runs? Got the ills?
Try a packet of Hackett's pills!"

Uncle Miles bent double when he'd told his verse, and I was fixing to bust. "Alexander, as you're finished with your breakfast, be off," Mother said.

"So will I," Dad said. And in a quiet voice he re-

36

marked, "Do your best with the front porch, Uncle Miles."

"How's that, Joe? Oh yes. I'll strip off anything I see with woodworm or dry rot. But don't count on comin' home to any Roman temple. Nelly Melba and I may lay off in the middle of the afternoon and go out to Snake Creek to see if the croppy is bitin'. After all, you can't do but so much when a house begins to pass out of fashion." He gave us all a wicked gum-grin and the three of us crowded out of the dining room, leaving Mother slumped in her chair.

❦ 5 ❧

DAD ENJOYS AN ANTONIO Y CLEOPATRA
cigar every morning and concentrates on it in the open
air. No smoking allowed at home. We walked along
part way together. "Your great-uncle Miles is a fine old
feller. I hope I'm out and about at his age," Dad said
finally, sounding pensive.

"He kind of sticks in Mother's craw," I observed.

"Who don't?" remarked Dad. "Everybody has their
different ways. But remember this, Alexander—Uncle
Miles is known as an honest man if he is a plain speaker.
And he'll give an honest day's work, though not even
your mother could overwork him. Lord, I don't know
what she's got up her sleeve for Lucille's party. You in
on any of that yet?"

"Not me."

"Well, anyway, Uncle Miles is a man who's lived just
the way he's wanted to. Can't many say that. I can't."

38

It was time for me to cut off in the direction of school. But I watched Dad walking away down Eldorado Street to his office, not hurrying because his shoes were tight. He didn't walk as upright as Uncle Miles, who has forty years on him.

The bell went before I was in the schoolyard. So I had to cut along in order to be at my desk before Miss Winkler started counting noses.

In the light of day, I couldn't quite put my finger on the state of mind the barn had put me in the night before. And that reminded me I'd forgotten to take breakfast to Trixie. With all this, it nearly slipped my mind I had a score to settle with Blossom Culp. I sat a few seats behind Blossom, but I could see her spider legs hooked behind her.

Most of the girls pull their hair back in big shiny ribbons, plaid or solid colors. But Blossom's was tied back with a length of string. She was a sorry sight, but clean.

"The monitor for row three is . . . ah . . . Alexander Armsworth!" Miss Winkler announced.

I hate being monitor, but I guess Miss Winkler thinks everybody has to take a turn. "Front and center, Alexander! And hands out for inspection!" Miss Winkler is no-nonsense about inspections. She looks over the monitor. Then the monitor looks over his row. Everybody has to be in order before we can go on to the Pledge of Allegiance and "The Star Spangled Banner."

"There are dingy halfmoons of soil beneath your fingernails, Alexander. A fine example for a monitor. Did you not have a good wash this morning?"

"No, ma'am. Lucille was in the bathroom for quite a time."

"Hmmm. Well, Alexander," she said quite loud, "when you cannot get into the bathroom to practice good hygiene, then go outdoors and wash under the pump."

We don't have anything as old-time as a pump, but it seemed showy to tell Miss Winkler that. And useless. I did have a clean handkerchief which she unfolded. And a pocket comb. So I got two out of three. I started down the row. Les Dawson's hands were filthy. But I didn't let on since he made a fist and shook it at me under the desk. When I came to Blossom, she put out her hands until every one of her finger tips touched mine. I drew back, and she drew forward. Girls don't have to have pocket combs, but they need to have fresh handkerchiefs, same as the boys. "Handkerchief?" I asked her.

She looked troubled and started reaching down and exploring inside the front of her middy blouse, though I knew she didn't have anything down there. But I took this as an opportunity.

"So just what were you up to last night?" I whispered at her.

"You seen something?" she said with surprise all over her face.

"I saw what you put there so I'd think I was seeing the Unseen," I mentioned in a somewhat confused way.

Blossom looked blank.

"I found that wet dog up there which you penned in the barn."

"I never been in that barn in my life and wouldn't go," she said out loud, which caused Miss Winkler to approach on my unprotected rear.

"You been up there twice to my certain knowledge," I hissed at her. "Once to plant that dog and late last night burning candles. Just to make me think I'm seeing—"

Blossom looked scared. That's the last I noticed of her before Miss Winkler's hand fell on my shoulder.

"This is *not* the social hour, Alexander!" This brought on a laugh from the class who don't socialize with Blossom at any time. "What is the nature of this unnecessary conversation?"

"She doesn't have her handkerchief," I betrayed.

"I see," said Miss Winkler. "But is that any reason for you to be holding hands with her?" How that had happened I don't know, but I jerked my hands away. "Blossom, have a clean handkerchief tomorrow or else. And if there is more raucous laughter in this class we will all be here till five o'clock. Work your row, Alexander."

So that's how it came to pass that I walked Blossom home for the second day running. But I thought it was my duty to because burning candles in the barn could set it afire and the Mercer with it, not to mention Trixie. Which I told Blossom in strong terms.

"Why, you even know my room looks out on the barn," I told her.

"I don't stand in your yard looking up at the windows. I don't go no place at night."

I argued with her all the way home. And now I know why. Because if it wasn't Blossom's doings, then maybe I was receptive and actually could see things other people can't. I decided to march Blossom up to the loft and confront her with the evidence, meaning Trixie and probably tallow drippings from the candle.

But Blossom set her brakes when she heard where we were going. "I don't mess with the Spirit World," she said. But I had her by the upper arm, marching her across our lawn. Uncle Miles wasn't in sight, but some of the wood gingerbread was off the porch and scattered like bones around the yard.

"Listen, Alexander, I don't want to go up in the barn. My mama wouldn't like it. She'd say some things is better left untampered with. She'd—"

"Your mama talks a lot," I said and gritted my teeth to show determination. When I threw back the barn doors, Blossom really dug in her heels. "No, I ain't going in," she said, closing those big eyes and shaking her head. "Besides, it ain't right, going up a haymow with a boy. I ain't like *Lucille*."

Now that really made me mad. I pushed Blossom ahead of me up the loft steps. But she snaked around, and I ended up dragging her. We both fell against the door and finished in a heap by Mother's old dress form. Seemed like I was forever falling down with Blossom's arms around me.

"Ohhhh," she said, "I don't like it up here. Where's that dog?"

I called Trixie and looked all over for her. I even went through the trunks. The coffee can of water and last night's hambone were there, looking untouched. Her orange crate had an unslept-in-look. I was set on finding that dog, though. Blossom wandered around the room, keeping her eye on the door.

"Why's it so wet up here?" she asked presently. The place did look damper than before. There was green slime and puddles. "It's like swamp water," Blossom said and stopped exploring.

I went on looking for a while even when I knew Trixie was gone. But my eyes were stinging and moist. And the only cover for that is rage. "Dad-rat you, Blossom Culp! Bringing a dog in here and then taking her away. That's a mean thing to do. I wanted to keep her!" Then I hiccupped, and a tear rolled down my cheek.

"Alexander," she said, soft and straight, "I never been up here in my life, and that's the truth."

"What about that time you claimed you were a Siamese twin?" I yelled. "Was that the truth too?"

"No," she said, looking at the floor behind me. "That was when . . . that was different. Alexander, let's go right now."

"What's the hurry?" I didn't know what to think, and I needed time. Blossom may not have any powers, but she's not bad at persuasion.

"Alexander," she said, "I'm begging you. Let's go." She was looking past me, and that made me turn around.

There on the floor behind me was a footprint. A perfect shape of a foot, including the toes—a girl's probably. Black with water and green with slime. I whirled around to see if Blossom had her shoes and stockings on. She did.

I turned back to the footprint which had soaked into the softwood floor but kept its shape.

"How'd you get your shoe and stocking off and back on without me seeing?" I barked in a jumpy voice. But when I tried to confront Blossom, she was gone. I heard her shoes banging down the steps.

And I followed without delay.

❧ 6 ❧

LUCILLE WAS HAVING A COMING-OUT
party. She wanted to have it before her class had their
graduation picnic, so nobody would confuse the two
events. As it turned out, nobody did.

It seems like that whole month of May was given
over to getting ready for it. It wasn't slated to be any
everyday kind of party. I was passing the time keeping
clear of both the barn and Blossom. I gave up hoping
to see Trixie again.

But Uncle Miles and I both got drawn into the
party preparations, though neither one of us cared
much for the work. A coming-out party, as far as I
could determine, was supposed to launch a girl into
polite society by putting her on display. Mother and
Lucille talked a good deal about launchings and coming
outs when they weren't arguing with each other. It
pretty much had me stumped. Because if Lucille kept
up with Tom Hackett on the porch settee much longer,
she'd be so far out she'd never get back.

Anyway, Mother hired extra help just to polish the silver. And she interviewed a baker on the subject of petit fours. The invitation cards were ordered engraved from a St. Louis firm.

"If it rains, I'll kill myself," Lucille often remarked.

When they told Uncle Miles he was to build a lattice-work pavilion on the lawn for serving refreshments from, he had a good deal to say. Then when Mother told him that all the best people serve lawn-party refreshments from a pavilion, he told her a number of things about the best people she didn't want to hear.

One of the things he pointed out was that the Van Deeters never accept invitations from people they don't receive. Which turned Mother's cheeks to chalk. But Uncle Miles reckoned the Hacketts would come since they'd feel obligated. And why not pass around a silver tray of laxative pills just to make them feel at home?

Then he got down to work, pounding laths into latticework all over the back yard. I helped him after school. As far as I can remember, Dad spent that whole month of May at his office, only slipping back home after dark.

We had our hands full with all the preparations. But the only part I enjoyed was working outside with Uncle Miles, though he did fuss at me quite a bit for not driving straight nails. Inside the house was a regular hell after the dressmaker took over in there.

One time Uncle Miles and I were working late. We were trying to finish up the long back pavilion wall and had it stretched out flat on the lane right in front of the barn doors. The sun was down, and I felt edgy that near the barn. I'd as soon have been up at the house.

"You believe in ghosts, Uncle Miles?"

"What brought that to mind all of a sudden?" he wanted to know. But I noticed he laid down his hammer and took out a plug of tobacco.

"Oh—I was reading a book—a library book—of ghost stories, and I just wondered if you maybe had an opinion."

Uncle Miles took two nails out of his mouth to make room for the plug. "Well, I am no hand at reading," he said, settling back against the hitching post. "But I don't hold with written-down ghost stories anyhow. They leave a person with the idee you have to have castles and dungeons and like that to attract a ghost. A lot of them stories are German anyway, so you got to take that into account. Some of them is English too. So you want to take into consideration that they're the products of two pooped-out peoples."

He worked his jaws in silence for a while, getting the plug into a chewable shape. I knew the day's work was at an end. "No," he said, "I wouldn't put any stock in made-up stories, especially them that claim to have took place in ancient days gone by. But of course there is ghosts."

It was evening then, and the katydids were starting up their whine in the Dutch elm. The latticework stretched out in the lane was glowing a sickly white.

And the barn towered over us. Nothing moved but Uncle Miles's jaws as he chewed.

"Naw," I told him. "There aren't such things as ghosts."

"Don't say what you don't know. I bunked in with a feller who seen one to his sorrow."

"Naw," I said hopefully.

"Boy, I don't lie."

Then he told me the story.

"Oh, it was twenty years ago and being restless I took off for the southern part of the state. Had a job down there at Teutopolis as drayman for the Star Store. I was weary of carpentry for a time and wanted a change.

"At the boarding house where I put up was a feller name of Cleatus Watts. He'd lost his best friend during an epidemic of the swamp fever which could be very bad down there at that time. People dropped like flies, laid in a coma, and flickered out.

"Anyhow, they'd buried Cleatus's friend a month before I come to town. And one time Cleatus come back to his room late. And there stood his friend in the room, facing away from the door. Why, for a minute it seemed so natural that Cleatus forgot the feller was dead. Then when he got his wits about him, he was in the room alone.

"He come down the hall and told me about it, and I said he was being fanciful.

"Well, the next night it was the same story. Cleatus

48

come into his room, and there the ghost of his departed friend stood, facing away from Cleatus and in a great anguish. The ghost was as real as the living man, Cleatus said. And it was tearing its hair and clawing the air something pitiful.

"Cleatus hotfooted it down to my room again, but when we went back, the ghost was gone, though the room smelled something wicked. Cleatus said that this sort of thing was getting on his nerves and did I think he ought to take lodgings elsewhere.

"I told him no, since the ghost of his friend was appearing to him for some purpose and would likely follow wherever he went. Cleatus took no comfort in this but saw the sense of it.

"Well, sir, third night running the ghost returned. And I tell you, I heard it myself. I was in bed but awake and heard Cleatus go into his room. There was quiet then, but I smelled graves.

"Then a voice I never heard before echoed down that hallway like a bell pealing. 'Turn me over, Cleatus!' it said. I can hear it yet. 'IN GOD'S NAME, TURN ME OVER!'

"Cleatus come pounding down the hall, half wild. But I stepped out and told him I'd heard it too, which was some relief to him. Why, that voice raised everybody in the place. There was a head poked out of every door and witnesses a-plenty.

" 'But what can he mean?' Cleatus says to me, grabbing hold of my arm like a child. 'What does TURN ME OVER signify?'

"I didn't know the answer to that one. But a bunch of us in the boarding house lit a lamp and went downstairs to the dining room table to put our heads together. The landlady set in with us, very concerned that her place might develop a bad name.

"It was her idee to take this problem to another woman who lived down there right outside of town. She sold herbs and root-mixtures and was otherwise a woman of wisdom. So that night Cleatus slept on the floor of my room, and the next day all of us paid this woman a call, a very dried-up old party but highly respected.

"She heard us out and nodded like she knowed where to put her finger on the problem. 'Get an affidavit from the county coroner,' she said, 'and have your friend's grave dug up and opened.'

"Some of us didn't like the sound of that and didn't see the point to it, but Cleatus was takin' the whole thing so bad we thought it couldn't hurt.

"Well, the coroner was under the influence of this wise woman anyway and oversaw the diggin' up of the grave personally. Of course, we all went along, wanting to get to the bottom of it.

"I don't know," Uncle Miles interrupted himself. "The rest of the story's grim. I don't know if you want to hear it."

I explained to him that I did.

"They dug down to the coffin and cleared the dirt off the top. And the first thing we all seen was that the nails on the lid was all wrenched loose. A gasp went up at that. And it was an easy matter to lift up the lid."

Uncle Miles paused a minute and ran his old knobby hands over his eyes. "When they got the lid off, we all seen the problem. The dead man was a-layin' face down in his coffin with his arms throwed back behind him."

"You mean—"

"That's right. What with the swamp fever panic and all, they hadn't let the body cool. And they'd buried him alive. He must have come to hisself underground. And I reckon it drove him mad and he thrashed around before the air in the box give out."

"What happened then?" I whispered.

"Well, the damage was done, wasn't it? They turned him over. I won't tell you what he looked like in the face. He'd eaten off his mouth. Then they nailed the lid on good and shoveled back the earth. He rested easy then. Cleatus Watts took it severe. The ghost never come to him again. But Cleatus started goin' to revival meetings and church twice of a Sunday, and was just generally not very good company thereafter."

"I think I better be getting up to the house, Uncle Miles. It's late."

"Well, that's enough for one day, I reckon," Uncle Miles said. But I was already halfway to the back door by then.

❧ 7 ❧

MOSTLY TO DRIVE MOTHER HALF OUT OF her head with worry, Uncle Miles didn't knock the latticework pavilion together till the morning of Lucille's party. We had it all done but the sinking of the posts to hold it up. Mother had driven stakes in the yard to show us just where the thing was to stand. And Uncle Miles was enjoying himself no end.

"I never been to what they call a party, Alexander," he said to me. "But I take a lot of pleasure in watchin' what folks put theirselves through to lay on a big show. Your maw, though, she takes the cake!"

"Well," I replied, "I guess she wants to give Lucille a good coming out."

"Many a big battleship has sank at its launching," said Uncle Miles who has never seen an ocean.

We had the sides up by midmorning on that sunny Saturday. Then Uncle Miles sent me up a stepladder to stretch a striped canvas awning over the top. He'd had the idea to fly a couple of American flags from the highest part. But Mother said she was having a party not a circus. Uncle Miles mentioned that on the whole he preferred a circus.

From the top of the pavilion I had a good view of the property. I was getting to the point where I could look at the barn without visualizing pink halos and burning candles. There was a brushpile between the barn and the streetcar tracks which was there because we'd picked the lawn clean. And I saw somebody lingering back behind it. It didn't give me much of a start. I dropped the hammer, but I didn't fall through the awning.

"Who's that over yonder?" I yelled out, and Uncle Miles looked pretty sharp through his spectacles.

At that, Bub Timmons stepped from behind the brushpile and said hey to both of us. I was surprised to see Bub who isn't one to drop by and was looking especially hangdog. Bub is the one who's still learning the mechanic's trade at the Apex garage. I thought maybe he'd stopped by to admire our Mercer as interested people will.

Bub is a good fellow, though not forthcoming in his conversation. He's had a rough row to hoe on account of his father, Amory Timmons. Who, if it hadn't been for my dad, would have had worse reason for grief than he did.

Amory Timmons worked as a common laborer all his life. He lost a hand while laying track on the Wood-lawn Avenue extension of the Bluff City Surface Lines streetcar company. It happened while they were just finishing off the trestle over Snake Creek out near the end of the line. It was the end of the line for Amory's hand.

He slipped and fell in new loose gravel just as a workmen's car came down the track. He'd have been cut in two if he'd moved slower. But the end of it was that the flanged wheel caught him just at the wrist. Witnesses said Amory's hand fallen there on the far side of the rail clenched up and shook. But witnesses will say a good deal to make a long story out of a short happening.

After that, everybody thought Amory would not be fit to do any kind of work and would have to live off the county. But my dad went to him and offered him a job in construction. Amory said he was useless, but Dad convinced him he could mix mortar and make cement one-handed, and Amory found he could. So he had steady work.

But still, ever after, Amory was given to bitterness against the streetcar company and went into states of mind that even liquor wouldn't touch. His wife and Bub told it around that Amory would get down at the foot of his bed some nights and bark like a dog. There were people who said he was a public menace, and they proved to be right. But Dad said he could do a good day's work when he wasn't low in his mind.

When I called out from the pavilion top, Bub walked

right up to us and spoke without preamble, as the saying goes.

"My pa is took especially bad," he said to me. "And Ma told me to skin over here and get word to your pa that he'll be off work for several days."

"Is he barkin' in his bed again?" Uncle Miles wanted to know.

Bub shook his head and fidgeted. "Worse," he said. "He's out in the creek bottoms crashin' through the underbrush and actin' wild."

"Had we ought to send out a party and bring him in?" Uncle Miles asked.

"No, nothin' comes of tryin' to deal with him when he goes off wavin' his stump and cussin' the streetcar company. Better to let him run loose till he comes to himself."

Uncle Miles nodded. And I told Bub I'd get word to Dad. Then Bub went on his way, heavy-laden with troubles. "A pitiful situation," Uncle Miles said, "and no two ways about it."

Then we turned back to our handiwork, the pavilion, which was up and looking very stylish but bare.

"The wonder is," said Uncle Miles, "that Luella— your maw—don't command a stand of rose bushes to grow up around that thing in time for the party." Then he marched off and untied Nelly Melba from the hitching post, climbed in his buggy, and was gone.

When Gladys called me in to noon dinner, I found

Mother and Lucille making a whole batch of paper roses. They were at the dining-room table rolling up pink and green crepe paper and were in a fine old sweat. "These are to be stuck in the sides of the trelliswork on the pavilion, Alexander," Mother said, waving a rose at me but never looking up.

They were cutting it pretty fine with those paper flowers, since the company for the party was due in three hours. But I guess with all the things they had to do, they'd naturally be working at something right down to the wire.

"As quick as you've had something to eat," Mother said, "I want you to arrange these roses on the pavilion and not just any old way. Put them in nice and don't bother about the back wall which won't show. It doesn't look like rain, does it?"

Lucille moaned. She was sitting there rolling up roses that looked like a lot of wadded paper to me. Her hair was done special, high on her head, and she was wearing her old wrapper. The ribbons on her corsets were poking out from her busts. I knew she hadn't eaten anything since Friday noon in order to get into her coming-out dress.

I had my dinner off the sideboard. And before I finished it, Mrs. Wysock came in the room, holding up Lucille's dress which was a mass of roses and ribbons. Mrs. Wysock is the dressmaker and usually pretty quick with her mouth. But she was keeping silent that day because she knew any little thing could set Lucille off into hysterics. She was right there on the edge.

Mrs. Wysock wanted to know where she could put the dress so it would hold its shape till time to put Lucille in it. Mother studied a while and then remembered her old dress form. And so she sent me to the barnloft to fetch it, though she had to tell me twice.

Venturing up the barnloft at high noon should not have been any big event for me. Still, I had to reason with myself somewhat. And just as I got to the barn doors, a cloud came across the sun that worried me worse than it would Lucille. It was like evening on the steps. I pushed the loft door open and made a quick grab at the dress form without looking around any.

But out of the corner of my eye I saw a girl's green skirt-tails brush across the floor and whisk into a corner behind a pile of boxes. I knocked the dress form down instead of getting a grip on it. When I reached down to pick it up, I figured Blossom was hiding up there and had nipped out of sight.

I'd wanted to think right along that Blossom passed her time up there. But I didn't stay to flush her out. If I'd caught a glimpse of her face, it might have been different. But as it was, I decided to leave and think about it.

So I hightailed it back to the house with the dress form, which was bigger than I was and shapelier.

I knew this party meant I'd have to take a bath and

put on a high-collared shirt. So I took my time poking the roses into the pavilion and setting up a plank table in there for the punch bowl. Every once in a while, I'd glance up to the barn window, but it seemed to be blank. I was trying to think of something smart I could do to let Blossom know I was on to her. When I was down to my last paper rose, the idea came to me.

I went up to the house for a pencil and a piece of paper from Gladys's grocery pad. The kitchen was full of big trays of small iced cakes with sugar roses on them. There was a dusky-looking woman with gold crosses hanging down from her ears. She was arranging the cakes on platters. She shot me a narrow look from her black eyes but never said anything.

I printed a note very careful on the top sheet of the pad. Then I ripped it off and ran down to the barn with it and the rose. This time I pounded up the stairs, making extra noise. Right in the middle of the floor up there where it couldn't be missed, I laid the rose down and the note with it. This is what it said:

> Here's a blossom for you, Blossom,
> you spidery-legged little spook.

I was pretty sure Blossom would rise to that. And if she had any good sportsmanship about her, she'd wear the rose tucked in her shirtwaist Monday at school. I was well pleased with myself for this cleverness.

❧ 8 ❧

NOBODY HAD TOLD ME I WAS TO PASS
NOBODY HAD TOLD ME I WAS TO PASS
the refreshments at this event. Mother saved that news
till the last minute. Then she poured salt into the wound
by hauling out a Buster Brown collar and told me I
was to put on my Sunday knicker suit including the
coat. Which is wool.

Mother's idea was for us all to receive the guests on
the porch and then invite them to wander down to the
pavilion where they'd refresh themselves with fruit
punch and cakes.

Down there Cousin Elvera Schumate was to ladle the
punch into little cups. And I was to circulate, offering
seconds on the cakes. The reason I had to do this, said
Mother, was that neither Gladys nor the extra help
were presentable enough to be seen. She must have
made this known in the kitchen, too, because Gladys
was out there pining away with her feelings seriously
hurt.

We began to assemble on the front porch before three o'clock because company in Bluff City are always right there on the dot if they're coming at all.

Dad said he was going to have one of his Antonio y Cleopatra cigars as we were on the porch, not in the house. Mother said he wasn't. She asked him how he thought she looked, and he stepped back to get a good view of her. She was uninterrupted ruffles with up at her throat a cameo as big as a saucer. Dad told her she looked just like the girl he'd married in 1892. So then she let him smoke his cigar but told him to flip his ash over the porch balustrade.

Lucille banged through the screen door, all in pale pink, carrying a bouquet of rosebuds with streamers. She was very low-necked and the top part of her outfit moved up and down with her breathing.

Mother told her she looked just like the duchess of York, but younger. Lucille returned the compliment by remarking that Mother looked just like Queen Alexandra, but younger. And Dad wondered aloud what was wrong with good American people.

"You look right miserable, Dad," I told him.

"So do you, Alexander, but younger," he replied.

The first person up the lane was Cousin Elvera Schumate. You could see her at quite a distance. There was a glass-eyed bird on her hat ready to take flight. She carried a walking stick with a tassle, though she is in no way lame.

When she drew nigh the porch, she looked up and

said, "Well, if you four aren't a fine-looking group of people suitable to receive anybody!"

Mother told her to join us on the porch before she had to ladle punch because she was family too.

At the stroke of three an automobile turned out of Pine Street and came up the lane at a stately pace.

"Dear Lord," said Mother, "That is the Van Deeters' limousine. Lucille, you have arrived."

Lucille was interested, but her mind was more on the Hacketts, on account of Tom. But getting the Van Deeters was icing on the cake.

So it was a bad moment when the limousine drew up to the porch steps with no Van Deeters in the back seat. The chauffeur, who wore gaiters, hopped out and darted up the steps to Mother, tipped his cap, and said, "Mrs. Van Deeter sends her compliments and a note." He was back in the driver's seat before Mother could get her fingers to work open the envelope.

Inside was a letter from Mrs. Van Deeter regretting that she had a previous engagement and wishing Lucille well. That was the only time I ever heard my Mother blaspheme, though it was only a small oath at that. And it was directed against Uncle Miles, not any of the Van Deeters.

By then, though, people were beginning to straggle up the lane, some horsedrawn and some by automobile. The younger ones of Lucille's crowd came on foot. Lucille waved her bouquet at them until Mother told her not to.

It seemed like the lawn just filled up with people all of a sudden. As they mounted the porch steps and passed along us, Mother would say, "You know our daughter, Lucille, of course." And everybody agreed.

Mother had to look at Lucille severely pretty often because she kept craning her neck trying to catch sight of the Hacketts. Lucille even took to whispering to me, though she is not in the habit of confiding in my direction.

"I know Tom's coming," she muttered, "because he gave me his word on it. But if his folks come too, then that's a sign they know he and I are—serious and they put their stamp of approval on it."

I was not sure I followed Lucille's reasoning, since people have been known to attend a party out of nothing but curiosity. But I supposed she had it all worked out in her own mind.

Mother was surveying the crowd pretty sharp too and would occasionally poke Dad and say things like, "Here come the Breckenridges and there are the Hochhuths behind them, so be on your best behavior." But Dad is pretty much on the same kind of behavior regardless of the company he's in.

Mother gave me the nod to start around the crowd with the iced cakes. I was just heading down off the porch when a big white and gold automobile turned into the lane. When it got closer, Dad said, "Why that's a new six-cylinder Coey Flyer touring barouche." When it got closer still Mother said, "Dear Lord, it's the

Hacketts." When it rolled to a stop, Lucille sagged. In it was Mr. and Mrs. Hackett, but not Tom.

"Hey there, Joe!" Mr. Hackett called out to Dad from the lane.

And Dad said, "Hey there, Walter," back to him. But when Mrs. Hackett climbed down out of the Coey Flyer, she kept her head over on one side and seemed not to take too much notice of anything. She wasn't dressed quite like the other women. She had on a big hat, though it was plain, and she carried a little tiny pocketbook on a chain.

"Oh, I guess that dress came from Chicago. It's very smart," Mother whispered sadly. And she made a gesture like she was trying to flatten out some of her ruffles.

Dad and Mr. Hackett go back a long way together as they pointed out to each other. But Mrs. Hackett was quite cool and passed off the porch with record speed, just glancing into Lucille's bouquet and smiling a small amount. Mother told me to conduct her personally down to the pavilion and Cousin Elvera. Mrs. Hackett took my arm and nodded a bit to people we passed. She asked me if I thought this was an amusing party, to which I didn't know how to reply. It was about to get amusing, but I did not foresee that.

Dad and Mr. Hackett were old friends together. It wasn't long before they had their coats off and their cuffs turned back to poke around under the hood of the Hacketts' new Coey Flyer.

I was in front of the snowball bushes by the porch

trying hard to rid myself of the rest of the cakes. I heard a rustling down near the ground. The thought of Trixie came to me, so I set the cake platter on the grass and parted the branches.

There was a quaint face looking out at me from under the porch, but it wasn't Trixie's. It was Blossom's. She was hunkered down out of sight, having a view of people's feet.

"You are everywhere at once, aren't you, Blossom?" I said to her. We were both down on our knees and nose to nose.

"I just wanted to have a look at what was going on," said Blossom "and kindly don't tell my mama." Then she darted a look past me at the platter of cakes.

"How would I have the chance to do that?"

"Well," she said, "she's working out in your kitchen this afternoon, piling the cakes on the trays." So then I knew who the woman was with the gold crosses in her ears who looked at me with the same black eyes as Blossom's. And that was the same woman who said I was receptive to the Spirit World. It worried me somewhat. I offered Blossom the tray and she helped herself to three cakes, which cleaned me out.

She commenced to nibble around one of the sugar roses and before I could back out of the bushes darted her face forward and gave me a thank-you kiss on the mouth. It took me by surprise and had a strawberry flavor.

My luck being what it is, Lucille was mounting the

porch steps just then and had a clear view of this business behind the bushes. Looking down, she said very haughty, "Alexander! How disgusting and at my party too!"

So I told her that what I was doing under the porch was not a patch on what she did *on* the porch with Tom Hackett. Which set her face to crumpling, since Tom had not yet shown up.

As I was exiting from the snowball bushes, I saw a young fellow approaching the house on foot, but it wasn't Tom. This fellow was dressed like the rest in a stiff straw hat and a whipcord suit. But he was tending to drag his feet along the lane, and I could not place him.

Since I was free of my cakes and Blossom, I walked down to make him welcome. He said his name was Seaforth and that he'd been sent out by the *Pantagraph* newspaper to cover the party because the society editor was elsewhere covering a dog and pony show at Wood River.

He said he had rather cover prize fights and other events with some action to them. But as a cub reporter he had to take such assignments as he was given. I asked him if he was from around these parts, and he said no, he was fresh from two years at the new journalism school over at the University of Missouri. And if I would fill him in and put him wise to the local scene, he'd be obliged.

I thought this was a step up from passing cakes, and

this Seaforth was a good fellow who talked to you man to man. Besides, I thought I'd better do my talking then because when Mother found out the paper was writing up our party, she'd be all over him.

"This is your sister's coming-out party, as I understand it," said Seaforth, whose first name is Lowell. "Is she good-looking?"

"That is a matter of opinion," I told him, remembering that Blossom said girls of Lucille's type were going out of style. "But Tom Hackett seems to think highly of her."

"That's Hackett's Laxatives?"

"The same," I told him.

"Then I take it that everybody who is anybody is here today," Lowell observed.

"Very nearly," I said. "The Breckenridges and the Hochhuths and the Hacketts senior to name but a few."

"Well, I guess the upper crust of one town is very like another."

I said nothing to that, not knowing.

Lowell remarked that everyone there seemed to be fairly pleased with themselves. And then he said,

> A town that boasts inhabitants like me
> Can have no lack of good society.

I saw that was a verse and thought it was clever. But he said it'd been written before him by the poet Longfellow.

Lowell looked up at the house and strolled around a bit, viewing it from various angles. "They don't build like this anymore," he mentioned. "This is the old place where the sea captain or whoever hanged himself, isn't it?"

I admitted that but said Mother didn't like it commented on.

"Well, I guess it'd be easier to die in than live in, what with the upkeep," Lowell said, "no offense meant. I see you have kept on the barn. But I suppose your father will be thinking of pulling that down in favor of one of these new garages they're building now."

I told Lowell that was the best idea I'd heard all day and showed him to the punch pavilion.

It was right then that Lucille's party took a turn for the worse. Tom Hackett's own auto, a brown and buff colored Crane-Simplex open model roared up the lane at an immoderate speed, swerved onto the lawn, and came to rest in one of Mother's flower beds, narrowly missing four girls from the high school. Tom Hackett stood up in the seat and then toppled out over the door, drunk as a skunk.

❧ 9 ❧

THE DAY JUST SEEMED TO GO DOWNHILL after that and continued to do so long after dark. Mother shrieked out that she'd have the law on whoever had torn up her flowers, before she saw it was Tom. He was face down among the begonias for a time and not identifiable.

His mother recognized his car, though, and left at high speed, taking Mr. Hackett senior with her. Others stayed on, interested to know what would happen next.

Tom was shortly on his feet and weaving toward the pavilion. He got there just as Cousin Elvera was telling Mrs. Hochhuth she had not seen so many well-dressed people in one place since the St. Louis World's Fair. Then Tom was before her, flush-faced, with loose earth caking his lapels.

"Say, listen, Mrs. Schumate," he bawled at her, "it's my opinion that whatever pink punch you're serving would profit by a little sparking up!" While he spoke, he was unscrewing the lid off a silver hip flask and pouring whiskey into the punchbowl with an unsteady hand.

There for a minute you could have made a photograph because nobody moved. Then Cousin Elvera screamed out, "You have poisoned my punch, and I don't care if you *are* Tom Hackett, I will not have it adulterated!" Or words to that effect.

She grasped the bowl in both hands and tipped it forward, and the punch cascaded right down Tom Hackett from his vest to his shoetops. Then Cousin Elvera fell back, and the bird on her hat took a dip.

"Things are picking up," Lowell said to me. "Is that the Hackett dude?"

"Where is my sweet—my sweet—has anybody seen Lucille?" Tom yelled out, stumbling in a circle with his wet trousers clinging to his legs.

Lucille was up on the porch with Mother's arms wrapped tight around her, and both were weeping copiously. Lucille had abandoned her bouquet on the porch rail, and it toppled into the snowball bushes, no doubt catching Blossom square on the head.

When Tom could focus on Lucille, he started in her direction. The crowd made way for him. It was then that Lowell Seaforth went into action. He strode up to Tom and took him by the arm. "Say, listen," said Tom. "You are asking for a flat nose or worse—do you know who I am?"

"Yes," said Lowell, "a common drunk," which brought forth a general gasp.

"Turn loose of me," Tom bellowed, "because I am going to my belov—my belov—I'm going up to greet Lucille."

"You won't be insulting any more ladies today," Lowell said in a voice that carried right up to the porch. Then he put a hammerlock on Tom's arm and marched him over to the Crane-Simplex which was axle-deep in the flowerbed. The crowd followed. He pushed Tom into the back seat where he seemed to pass out at once, though I think personally that he was playing possum. "Tell me where this boozer lives, and I'll drive him home," said Lowell. And after considerable maneuvering, Lowell got the Crane-Simplex out of its burial ground and spun off down the lane.

He had not turned into Pine Street, though, before Mother was asking who he was. When she learned he was a reporter sent to write up the story of the party, she forgot herself completely, shouting out, "We are publicly shamed and finished in Bluff City!"

Dispatching Tom Hackett so stylish was enough to make anybody an admirer of Lowell Seaforth. But what he wrote up for the next day's newspaper was another star in his crown. Though a good deal happened before the next day's *Pantagraph* even went to press, I'll put in Lowell's article right here where it fits best:

MISS ARMSWORTH BOWS TO SOCIETY

Mr. and Mrs. Joe Armsworth and son Alexander were at home to their numerous friends yesterday afternoon. *The lawn party began under sunny skies promising a bright future for Miss Lucille Armsworth, who takes her rightful place as an ornament of Bluff City social circles.*

The commodious grounds of the Armsworth mansion on Pine Street were the scene of a gathering drawn from the community's oldest families and enlivened by members of the younger set. All were handsome or beautiful in their attire.

A sudden dampness spelled a premature end to one of this season's most select occasions. Mrs. Elvera Schumate poured.

❦ 10 ❧

THEY SAY HISTORY REPEATS ITSELF, which can be nervewracking. Though in this case it was a good thing it did. I'm talking about candlelight in the barn.

We were a good while settling Lucille and Mother down after the party that night. Gladys took a supper tray upstairs to Mother, who said she could not face anybody anymore that night or maybe ever. Lucille was a worse case. She stalked through all the rooms staring up at the ceilings like she was planning to take her cue from Captain Campbell and hang herself from a light fixture.

She had pulled all the combs out of her back hair, which flowed freely. She was on a rampage for sure.

"How could Tom Hackett do such a thing to me?" she wailed numerous times.

And finally Dad said, "Tom Hackett was never my idea."

Which only set Lucille off again. "To arrive liquored-up at my party just when I thought—oh, I am ruined and it is too awful."

What Lucille thought was that she had Tom in her sights—and with witnesses. She had no doubt been planning an engagement party to follow her coming out. But Lucille was still thinking even in the midst of her rage. She has a practical side to her nature that comes out at odd moments.

Pretty soon she flopped in a chair and reasoned it out with herself. "Tom Hackett is crazy about me and has made it plain. But it was having to face up to the formalities of our families' meeting that made him—shy. So he just naturally had a little too much to drink so he wouldn't have to go through a—meaningless social ritual."

"A *what*—which cost me seventy-five dollars not counting the damage to the yard?" asked Dad.

"Never mind, Dad," said Lucille. "I am feeling better about it now."

"That is the first good news I have had these many months," Dad said. "Let's all call it a day."

"But I have some bad news, Dad," I had to say to him.

"Oh never say so, Alexander," he moaned. "What is it?"

"Bub Timmons was by this morning and said his pa was in a bad way and running out of control and not to look for him at work for a while."

73

"Alexander," Dad said, "that is a shame, but with what we have been through today, I'm not going to take it to heart." Then he led the way upstairs and I followed. Lucille, though, headed through the house in the other direction toward the back hall where we have installed the telephone.

I was in my bed, reviewing the day, which took quite a time. What was foremost in my mind was the way Lowell Seaforth had taken Tom over. You couldn't help but marvel at a fellow who would step up and take charge like that.

I listened to three, maybe four streetcars rattle by out back and was beginning to feel drowsy when I heard something else. It was way off at the front of the property, but I knew the sound of Tom Hackett's Crane-Simplex. All I could make out was the engine purring along, which must have meant he was driving on the grass to avoid the gravel. I was reminded then that I never had heard Lucille come upstairs.

She is going to make it up with him pretty quick, is what I thought to myself, before he has time to realize what fools he has made of them both. So, bye and bye, quite a while after I heard the car stop, I slipped out of my room and up to the spare bedroom right over the piazza. I like to listen in to other people's business, which is probably why I was not too sanctimonious with Blossom when I caught her under the porch watching our party.

The view out over the front lawn was not encouraging. It looked like a team of Clydesdales had dragged a road-grader across the grass, and paper roses were blowing everywhere. Tom and Lucille were in the settee directly below. No sound came from them at first except for the rustle of Lucille's dress and small sighs.

I was half asleep at my post when Tom said, "Have I made my girl unhappy?"

Lucille murmured something in reply. "I wouldn't do anything to hurt my girl. She knows that, doesn't she, because she is the sweetest, most generous girl in the world?"

Oh this is pretty disgusting, I thought to myself. More murmurs from Lucille.

"But what does it matter what other people think? At most times I can hold my liquor and I always sober right up," said Tom, gaining confidence. "My father could buy and sell everybody in town except maybe the Van Deeters who weren't even there to see me when I'd had a drop too much."

Oh, I thought to myself, I wish there was an extra bowl of punch I could fling down on their heads. "You know," said Tom, "my intentions regarding you are strictly on the up and up and as far as I am concerned we are already engaged, married even."

Oh, Lucille, you think you have him where you want him again, and it'd serve you right if you did, is what I thought.

"So let us have a kiss to show we aren't mad, and then some more," said Tom. Then later, "Yes, Lucille, but let's not rush into any public announcements until after you graduate from the high school. It wouldn't do if the word got around that I was robbing the cradle."

Then Lucille's voice came up quite strong. "You will not slip through my fingers, Tom Hackett," she said. "Never think it." Oh, this is more than I can stomach, I thought to myself, and crept off to my room.

I guess if the conversation passing back and forth between Tom and Lucille had not been so sickening, the whole history of Bluff City would be different. Because I would not have gone on back to my room when I did.

❧ 11 ❧

THE ROOM WAS SO BRIGHT I COULD AL-most make out the colors on my patchwork quilt. There looked to be a million lightning bugs glowing outside the window. I walked over to it and stared out to the barn. The dormer window was ablaze with candlelight. "Blossom is outdoing herself," I said. But the words stuck in my throat.

Why I didn't yell to raise the house I don't know. The light slanted down from the window and threw a long patch of yellow across the yard. It was all as quiet as a tomb. Then a flock of roosting birds stirred in the elm. They flapped their wings with a sudden noise and wheeled off into the night. So did I.

When I got out back, the birds were gone, but the light wasn't. I cut across the yard and fetched up by the hitching post, not thinking too far ahead. There beside the barn, I looked back at the long shape on the lawn, bright as electricity but not so white.

The barn door opened to darkness, but there was plenty of light leaking around the doorframe at the top of the stairs. It pulled me on like the moth to the flame. Oh, Blossom, I will wring your scrawny neck, thought I. Then I was in the loft and not alone.

There was a girl standing there, near enough to touch. I could see her plain, though the loft was not as bright as I expected. And no wonder, since there was not a sign of a candle. She was a girl about my age, working her hands in front of her. She had on an odd outfit. A long green dress right down to the floor. Toward the bottom, it was limp and dark, as wet as Tom Hackett's trousers. I studied this costume considerably rather than to stare fixedly into a face that was not Blossom's and never could be. Not Blossom in disguise. Not anybody I ever knew.

First a damp dog and now a damp girl, I thought, but did not say aloud since a lot of the spunkiness had left me.

Then the loft was full of her voice, though so quiet it could have come from inside my head. "My hoops!" this girl said, clutching at her sopping skirts. I looked right at her face. It was heartshaped and very woebegone. She put a hand up to her neck where there was a brooch of the old-fashioned kind. It looked to have a glass covering over flowers made of human hair, which was a decoration done in days gone by.

"My hoops, my hoops," she said looking through me. "I am lost. All is lost," she went on, and in an accent I could not place. Foreign, certainly. She was altogether such a novel type that I gained a little courage.

"What is your business here?" I challenged her. And this is the time when history decided my voice was to start changing. So what I really said was:

"*What is*
                        busi
            your
                                ness
                                        here?"

Then she looked at me, boring holes in my head with her eyes. "Oh!" she said, "The dead and the dying! The boilers gone, and the black water!" Her voice rose by the minute to a shriek. And just before she buried her face in her hands and her wet hair fell forward, she howled out, "THE DEAD ARE ROBBED AND CANNOT FORE-STALL IT!"

This is madness, I thought to myself and felt capable of running. I never moved, but she knew I would and put out a trembling hand that came too near touching me. "Stay," she said, very clear and low. "Time is nothing to me, and the past contends with the future. But I know you, even in my loneliness, though I was here before you."

"What is your name?" I croaked.

She looked surprised at that and quite human. "Why, Inez Dumaine," she said as if I should have the sense to know.

Then another change came over her, and she balled up both her fists to strike the air. She set to moaning, but somewhere off in the corner of the loft there was another noise, the sound of Trixie whining.

"More death!" she said in a heavier accent. "More, if you do not stop it. Others lost, like me in the black water. Save them!"

Wind began to blow through the loft, though the window is sealed. It was brighter everywhere except for Inez Dumaine, who darkened to a silhouette. I was wrapped up in a nightmare. And like in a dream, I only watched.

Her face was in shadow before she spoke again. "Listen to me, time matters to you. The bridge is a killer. The train—without a locomotive—the train will be lost. On the bridge. Stop it. The man with one hand. The tracks lead to . . . nothing."

Then her eyes blazed up like some creature at the side of a dark road. And I was standing down by the hitching post with my hand hanging onto the cold iron ring. The soles of my feet were sore from pounding down the stairs. The yard was dark, and the barn was darker. There was a twittering up in the tree where the birds were resettling. And all I had in my head were words.

More death . . . black water . . . the killer bridge . . . the train without a locomotive . . . the tracks that lead to . . . nothing . . .

And *the man with one hand.*

I darted past the brushpile behind the barn and barely

noticed there was a dim light from the Culps' kitchen beyond the tracks. I was right there between the rails on the trolley line with the wind whipping me when I remembered I was in my nightshirt.

Before I had to deal with second thoughts, a streetcar came rattling out from town. It made the turn a block away, and the headlamp beam swung around and caught me in the eyes. The car always speeds up after the curve, especially on the last run of the night. It kept coming, but I was rooted between the rails.

The motorman's outline stood up against the inside lights. But the headlamp was like Halley's Comet. I hoped the driver would see me clearer than I saw him. I did my best to flag him down with my nightshirt, which set me to dancing on the splintery ties. He commenced clanging his bell, which he never does on a late run.

I was so dazed by the light and recent experiences that I'd have let myself be run down. But the motorman set his brakes, and sparks sprayed out on the right of way. He was stretching out the side window and waving his fist.

Then he ripped out a couple of oaths. And said if I wanted a ride, I'd have two things to do. Put on some decent clothes and wait at the trolley stop like anybody else.

"There's trouble on the line," I told him, wondering if there was.

"There'll be trouble for you for making mischief!" I swung up into the car. He said that as I was entering, I had better have a nickel in my nightshirt. This brought a laugh from the passengers who stared at me a little like I had stared at Inez Dumaine. They all looked to be late workers or people who'd been to a show at the Empress Opera House.

"That is the Armsworth boy," somebody said, like I was a point of interest they were passing.

"Off, boy, before I drag you up to your house by the ears," said the motorman, a tough customer with big knuckles.

I got a good grip on the pole by the coin box. "Listen, there's something wrong on the trestle—over Snake Creek." This brought a few of the passengers to their feet. The motorman pushed his cap back and looked put upon.

"If this is a prank," he said, "your bottom will burn for it." But the passengers were crowding up front to see if they could read truth in my face.

One of them said, "Take it easy to the bridge and then have a look."

"Siddown, all of you'uns, especially *you*," he nodded to me. "You'll have a free ride and a long sorry walk back if you're a liar." Under the circumstances, I figured this was fair enough, though the vision of Inez was fading fast under the glare of this motorman. Here was a man who would never believe anything told to him in a barnloft. The streetcar jerked once and rolled. I looked over my shoulder out the window, across to Blossom Culp's back porch. Her mother was standing there, with her hair in a braid. She was holding a hurricane lamp up by her face, staring out into the night.

We hummed along a mile or so to where the town thins out. The motorman kept up a steady conversation with himself about his plans for me. And I tugged at my nightshirt which continually pinched in between the slats on the seat.

Then we were among the trees and high weeds along the creek bluffs, slowing to a crawl. The headlamp shone straight along the trestle. There were the two gleaming rails and the sheer black drop on either side. I lost considerable heart at the ordinariness of the view and wished I was back in my bed.

"Let's get out and have a quick look," said a rider. "Better safe than sorry." But as he walked to the front of the car, he gave me a look of deep suspicion.

Another passenger piled out behind him as people will to get in on something. But the motorman stuck to his place like I might make off with the streetcar and go Halloweening with it. We all watched the two of them walk out on the trestle, looking first on one side and then the other. I didn't see how a couple of middle-weights could test a bridge for a trolley car's weight. But then I figured I might have said too much already. So I composed myself in silence.

"What's that down there by the creek on this side?" yelled out one of the strollers to the other. Everybody in the car surged forward to see those two looking down a drop of maybe a hundred feet. Then they started back to the car, shading their eyes against the headlamp.

"There's a fire down there at the base of the bridge support," said one.

"A tramp's campfire, very likely," said the motorman, offhand.

"Amory Timmons's campfire if anybody's," I said out loud. That made everybody turn my way. I guess there wasn't a soul in the county who didn't know about Amory Timmons and his grudge against the streetcar company.

"What do you know about it?" said the motorman, taking a step in my direction.

"Amory Timmons is running wild in the creek bottoms," I said. "It's common knowledge."

"He goes crazy sometimes," one of the passengers said.

"All right," said the motorman like this is the last straw. "Let's shinny down the bluff and have a look. I'm not taking responsibility for this car if something irregular's going on." I doubt if he meant for everybody in the trolley to follow, but we did. There were about fifteen of us, including some courting couples who didn't mind a lark in the dark.

So we all scrambled over the gravel shoulder and started down into the treetops. It's steep going, but people were chuckling as they went. Some of the girls let out little squeaks. I trod on a stone that liked to lay my bare foot open. But after a few steep yards we came to a path that zigzagged down.

By then we could see where we were going. There was a fire below, and it was not for frying catfish. When we got near, it was licking up the side of one of the wooden trestle supports.

"My God!" the motorman said. Then he lost his footing, and there was the sound of small bushes giving out under him. A lot of smoke rose above the flames, and there was the stink of creosote used to treat the bridge wood. There was a smell of coal oil too.

"That fire was set a-purpose," the motorman said when he got on his feet. We kept threading down and down. There was no turning back what with everybody slipping and sliding the same direction. The flames were licking up higher, lighting up the whole underside of the bridge. I've been swimming there many a time. It was bright as day down on the sandbar, and somebody pointed. "Lookit right there—and there too!"

We looked. All the supports lit up by the fire looked to be hacked at with an axe. Some of them were cut through with raw white wood showing like pencil points. It'd taken a one-armed man a long time to manage it. He must have started at sundown and axed away while the earlier cars had passed over his head.

We stood there, all of us strangers, open-mouthed at the sight. The trestle was burning like tinder. Sparks and flaming splinters dropped off into the black water of Snake Creek which reflected the fire but couldn't quench it.

"The fire department— " somebody said then. And somebody else started to turn like he would run for help. But nobody really moved.

Then from the opposite side of the creek came a sound like a giant featherbed busting open—one big whooof. A billow of flame went up over the treetops, and there was a stronger whiff of coal oil. The whole far side of the bridge, higher up, broke into flames. One of the girls began to cry, but nobody comforted her. We were all transfixed.

"Well, it's done for," somebody said quietly.

"So quick," the girl sobbed, "Why, we might have—"

I guess we all saw the same thing at once, though my eyes were dancing with the flames. The other side of the bridge was wreathed around in fire. Even the ties were burning. And through that inferno a man ran.

I wonder now why we didn't all yell and point him out to each other. But we didn't. He was small in the distance, a black running figure, hopping along the ties right across the bridge, from one fire to the other. He was carrying a flaming torch, swinging it around and around as he ran. With the only hand he had.

All our necks craned up and all our eyes followed him across the trestle till he disappeared in between the bluffs we'd come from.

My pa is took especially bad, I could remember Bub Timmons saying not more than twelve hours before.

"Amory Timmons," the motorman said, "That crazy old son of a—"

"He don't know what he's doing," somebody murmured.

"I know it," the motorman said mournfully.

"We better try to catch him," came an eager voice. And like any mob, we all turned back to the path at once.

But then we heard a clanging over the crackle of the fire. The bell on the streetcar. It went on and on like a mad thing. And the car edged out onto the trestle. The flames were well up at this end of the bridge, and the streetcar's orange paint glowed like a sunrise. The girls began to shriek at that, and they wouldn't stop. I think I was shrieking myself. The trolley jerked across the trestle, picking up a little speed.

When it was above the first flames, we could see a man at the controls. His head was out of the window. And if we could have heard anything, I think we'd have heard him barking like a dog. Or laughing. I still think I saw a laughing face, though I was too far off to be sure.

One of the bridge supports cracked like a rifle. And the rest of them took up the report. "Get back!" the motorman yelled. "The whole thing's going!" We all scrambled backward, and I fell on the wet ground cover and crawled up the bank into the trees. As I clawed the earth, I could feel other people's hands doing the same.

If it hadn't been for the spectacle behind us, I guess we'd all have gone to ground like moles. But up among the ferns and willows I looked back, like Lot's wife.

The streetcar was still rolling toward the middle of the trestle. And the track was sagging. The car began to dip. The bell clanged and clanged in fury while the supports fell one after another into the creek, landing with smacks.

Then it all gave out. The trolley seemed to miss its footing and stagger. The rails under it looped like wire. And the car heeled over. For a second you could see the dark roof as the car pitched sideways in a hail of scattered ties. And Amory Timmons dropped out of the motorman's window. He fell the length of the flames, looking like a lopsided starfish, turning in the air.

The trolley went end over end and hit the fallen supports in the creek. It burst open like a crate.

And the bell ceased clanging.

❦ 12 ❦

I WALKED A MIDNIGHT MILE ON TROL-
ley track barefoot after that, with the sights and sounds
of death running through my mind.

It was an easy matter to get away from the little band
of watchers down by Snake Creek. The girls set up a
lamentation, and the men moaned and muttered. I
worked my way up through the brush, and no one
marked my leaving. When I got close to home, I was
walking mostly out of habit, and never gave the barn a
thought as I went by. All I wanted was my bed.

Shortly, I was flopped belly down across it, too worn
out to turn back the quilt. I was scared, but too tired to
taste the full flavor of it.

Then the door banged back, and the light went on.
I flipped over and pulled my nightshirt down. There
stood Lucille in the doorway, every nerve on end and
looking like the queen of tragedy. Her eyes were mean
slits.

"You repulsive little worm!" she rasped out. "You hateful little meddler! I've caught you at last!

What now? I thought to myself. This is entirely too much after a hard night. "Lucille—"

"Hush! Keep your voice down. This is between you and me!"

"Lucille," I said quieter, "I'll gladly plead guilty to whatever charges, but right now I'm a little tired and—"

"Guilty is the word!" said Lucille, making for my bed. "How dare you lurk up in that barnloft, spying, and in that ridiculous costume too! Tom Hackett bolted like a startled hare just when—I will kill you, Alexander, and that is a promise. You have ruined my last chance with Tom, and now you have a desperate woman to deal with."

My thoughts tried to keep apace with Lucille's mouth. But they were not equal to the task. They must have fallen somewhat behind because she presently had me by my nightshirt and was hissing dangerously in my ear, "Deny it if you dare and add lies to your loathsomeness!"

"Deny what, Lucille?"

"That you were in the barn. Look at your nightshirt —and your feet. They're filthy. You *were* in that loft tonight, weren't you?"

"I can't deny that, Lucille, but—"

"Ha!" said Lucille and gave me a shake.

"—but I was not up there when—anybody else was."

"A bald-faced lie!" she howled, forgetting to hiss.

"You went up there to meet that red-necked little arachnid creature from across the tracks. That *Blossom!* And here's the proof!" Lucille whipped out of her wrapper pocket the paper rose and the note I'd left, the one that said,

> *Here's a blossom for you, Blossom,*
> *you spidery-legged little spook.*

"Oh I saw you under the porch at my party. You're sweet on her, which is repulsive in itself. But up in the barn at night!"

Since Lucille and Tom had crept up the loft themselves, by her own admission, I did not think she had any business to be passing judgment on the doings of others. I told her this, which was a mistake. She fulminated something fierce, which gave me the time to remember one of her opening remarks.

"Hold on a minute, Lucille, before you work me over," I said, though my head was snapping back and forth from her shaking. "What is this about a ridiculous costume?"

"*You* have the nerve to ask, who devised the whole hellish scheme! You know perfectly well what I'm talking about. Rising up in the corner just as Tom and I— rising up in the corner in that nasty old green dress you must have dredged up out of a trunk—holding a candle under your chin to distort your features and giving us both such a turn—and sending us down the steps—I might well have fallen and broken my—and Tom making off into the night like a thing pursued—oh, Alexander, is there no limit to your spiteful perfidy?"

This disjointed account was clarifying somewhat. Evidently Tom and Lucille had been visited by the ghost of Inez Dumaine. Inez, I thought, Inez, you have been working overtime this night.

A great dismalness came over me. How could I explain to Lucille that she and Tom had been disturbed by a specter instead of me? Lucille lacks the imagination to follow that line of reasoning.

After a night of terror, I was pretty well resigned to dying at the hands of my own sister. But a voice from the door called out, "Lucille! Unhand him!"

She wheeled around, and I retreated to the far side of my bed. Mother and Dad stood in the doorway, looking like they hadn't just arrived. "Go to your room, Lucille!" Mother said. "Snuggling in the barnloft! Brawling in the house! Your party disfigured by that drunken oaf, Tom Hackett, who would ruin you and cast you to one side without a momentary qualm! That —*laxative playboy!* That you would so much as *contemplate* seeing him again after that party, much less allowing him to *lure* you into the barnloft! All your father and I, especially I, have done and all our well-meaning efforts came to this!"

Lucille looked in wonderment at Mother for an instant. Then she let out a screech and pounded from the room.

"You have saved your sister from a fate worse than death, Alexander, though your manner of doing so was rather showy. Nevertheless, one day she will thank you for it. But do not let those dirty feet of yours come in contact with the sheets. And go to sleep at once. It's past your bedtime!"

Mother turned on Dad then, like he might have contradicted her on some point. But he was clearly buffaloed by all the foregoing. Then in the distance came the sound of an ambulance bell. It rang from the direction of the Woodlawn Avenue extension. Out to pick up all that remains of Amory Timmons, I thought privately.

Mother harked at the far-off ringing, which has a calamitous sound, particularly at night. "And what tragedy does *that* portend?" she asked, very dramatic.

At that, the night breeze played up into a wind, lashing the elm branches around. A crackling sound came from the side yard, followed by the splintering of wood and a great crash. Dad unlatched the window screen and stuck his head out. Then he ducked back in and told us that Lucille's party pavilion had blown down.

Mother drew her wrapper around her neck and said darkly, "This night is full of omens."

I was inclined to agree.

As a rule, Sunday stands pretty still in Bluff City. Of course, that particular Sunday was an exception. I woke up looking at my dirty feet, a pair of souvenirs of a busy night. There was a nettle rash on my legs too, from all those weeds I'd come through climbing away from Snake Creek. It was just a question of time before some busybody would link me up with the salvation of the streetcar passengers. And when this revelation came, it would open up a whole new field of inquiry.

The smell of Gladys's coffee wafted up from the dining room. There was no way of avoiding church because there never is. The Baptists were already setting to in their chapel over on Eldorado Street, and their old pump organ was wheezing a prelude. They are hard-shell, but harmonious, and they raised up their voices in song: "Draw me nearer, O my savior, day by day." We have given up being Baptists in favor of being Episcopalians, which is a step up socially but a step down when it comes to hymn-singing.

Not wishing to be conspicuous until it was inevitable, I got into my Sunday clothes and started down to the dining room unbidden. Lucille was at her place, puff-faced, with the *Pantagraph* folded open to Lowell Seaforth's article beside her plate of waffles.

"There now," Mother was saying, "that nice young man from the paper did your party proud and omitted unseemly details, for which we owe him many thanks. It is up to you, my girl, to hold your head high and let the community know you are of a superior type who has seen the light regarding such people as the Hacketts."

Dad was doggoned if he knew how all of a sudden—

overnight so to speak—every one of the Hacketts had turned out to be such lowlifes. But he was given a couple of stricken looks and subsided.

I slid the newspaper out from under Lucille's elbow and read Lowell's article, thinking it was handsome of him to mention my name as one of the party-givers. Then I leafed to the front page for word of the trestle disaster, which was surely the biggest thing that had happened to Bluff City in living memory. But the news hadn't broken on that yet.

Gladys came in with my plate of waffles and remarked that the lawn looked like the Battle of Bull Run had been waged across it. At length, Mother said to Lucille, "Get your hat and gloves. You're going to church as usual." The fight was pretty much out of Lucille. She kept darting me looks that spoke strongly of possible gratitude and certain revenge. I could see she was still unsettled in her mind. For that matter, so was I.

We drove the Mercer to church, and Mother nodded to everyone on foot along the way. Lucille kept her veil down until the last moment before she had to take communion.

"Let us rejoice and be exceeding glad," said Father Ludlow in place of his prepared invocation, "that our brothers and sisters in this community were snatched from untimely and awful death."

There was a mumbling in the congregation by those who knew about the bridge business telling their neighbors. "And let us pray for our benighted brother, Amory Timmons, whose madness hath delivered him from our realm to the seat of a merciful judgment."

Dad stirred at that, but Jake McCulloch, the undertaker, leaned up from the pew behind and whispered into his ear. Then Dad slipped forward on the kneeler and offered a silent prayer for Amory's soul. I did the same, feeling bad that I hadn't thought of it before.

The thought of Inez Dumaine interrupted my prayers for Amory. I didn't know what to make of Inez, but I knew then as I know now that she is of the next world, not this, so I added a word or two in her behalf.

While I was doing all this praying, Father Ludlow was saying in the background, ". . . and a little child shall lead them." Though I am not exactly little and no longer a child, I took this as a personal reference. I could begin to feel the hot breath of publicity on the back of my neck. And I knew full well that I'd have some explaining to do of matters very difficult to explain.

❧ 13 ❧

I SPENT THAT LONG SUNDAY AFTERNOON down among the snowball bushes, somewhat bemused. Up in the house Mother and Lucille were going at it hammer and tongs. Lucille was complaining in loud terms about how Mother had been throwing her at Tom's head since she was in short skirts. And Mother was responding that she had always thought Tom was a ne'er-do-well, a feckless masher, and a poor prospect.

Lucille said that, as an opinion, this was a new one to her. And Mother answered that Lucille had always been susceptible and had no more sense of decorum and propriety than a barnyard fowl. She also quoted Uncle Miles's history of the Hackett family without giving him any credit. They went over this ground a number of times, and the snowball bushes muffled very little of the noise.

Along toward midafternoon, I spotted Lowell Sea-forth ambling up the lane with his straw hat on the back of his head. He looked weary, and I attributed that to his spending a sleepless night on the Snake Creek story. I parted the snowballs as he drew near the house.

"Well, Alexander," he said in some surprise.

If he'd come for a word with me, I said, he might care to join me in the bushes where there was some prospect of privacy. He replied that there are few places he won't go for good journalistic material.

Lowell made himself comfortable against the porch foundation and came right to the point. He said that certain of the streetcar survivors had mentioned my name. "I take it that word of this hasn't reached your family since I'm conducting this interview under the porch."

That was about the size of it, I told him. And as he is a first-rate newspaperman, it didn't take him long to learn from me that I was the same Alexander Armsworth who flagged the trolley with my nightshirt. When it came to modest heroes, Lowell said, looking up at the leaves, I took the cake. "Now, then, Alexander, just how did you know to give the alarm?"

When in doubt, tell the truth, as the saying goes. Though I never thought for a minute a fellow as worldly as Lowell Seaforth would credit a ghost in the barn and a message from the Great Beyond.

When he heard me out, he said, "Sure it wasn't some little neighborhood girl dressed up and playing the fool? Seems to me just yesterday right where we sit I saw a girl under these snowball bushes."

I told him that Inez Dumaine was definitely not Blossom in disguise, though I gave Blossom credit for informing me that I was receptive to the Unseen. "This is a tall tale, Alexander," Lowell said. "Let's us have a look at the barn."

We went around the house and under the shadow of the Dutch elm, fetching up beside the hitching post. Lowell examined everything pretty close, though I was in some question about how seriously he took my story.

"Captain Campbell built this place, didn't he?" I nodded, noticing that Lowell's brows were knitting. "Then why do you reckon he had these initials carved on the hitching post instead of his own?" I looked down at them as I had done many a time without thinking. I looked down at I.D.

"Inez Dumaine," Lowell said and looked at me with new eyes. I stared at the initials, and my throat went dry.

Lowell had a look up in the loft, but I hung around outside. He seemed to want to do his own investigating. He was up there quite a spell, and once when I started to lean an elbow on the hitching post, I thought better of it. Finally, he came back.

"Somebody's been up there pretty recently," he said. "There's a small wet footprint, though why there should only be one I cannot figure." I told him it was a regular feature of the place, and had he happened to see a small wet dog?

"No," said Lowell, "but nothing would have surprised

me. I am a skeptic regarding the supernatural, but there is nothing natural about that loft. Sure you didn't think up a name to go with those initials on that hitching post, Alexander?" he said, possibly to catch me off guard.

"I'm sure," I told him, and he believed me.

"I will tell you straight, Alexander," he said. "Amory Timmons and the trestle is a big story, bigger than I ever bargained for so early in my career. But when we add to it your ghostly tale, I wonder if it won't stretch the credulity of the readers."

I was not altogether sure what *credulity* meant, but I got the drift. "Well, if it is all the same to you, Lowell, why don't you keep me out of your story altogether?"

"I'm afraid that wouldn't do much good," he replied, "considering that rumors circulate faster than newspapers."

As proof of that, Mother came out on the back porch calling me. When she spotted Lowell, her eyes lighted up, but she was distracted. We drew near, and she looked from one of us to the other. "Oh, Mr.—"

"Seaforth," I said.

"Yes," said Mother. "We are deeply in your debt regarding the party yesterday, and I—have you met our daughter, Lucille?—won't you step inside and take some refresh—" Mother made several half turns and fanned the screen door. "Alexander, there are people out front mentioning your name. Your father is dealing with them, but he is hardly equal to it, and I think—oh, the two of you had better step inside." But she blocked the door for some time, trying to get her priorities in order.

We finally eased her through to the hall. From the other end of the house came a buzzing of voices. The only one I could make out was Dad's. He was saying, "As far as I know, Alexander was not off the place all last evening."

"You had just as well face your public," Lowell said to me, casting Mother into deeper confusion.

Then from the group of people in the front hall, the motorman stepped out, pointed his finger at me, and said, "That there is the boy!"

But he was pushed to one side by a girl with a number of flowers on her hat. I didn't recognize her, but she made straight for me and threw her arms around my neck.

"Now see here," Mother said.

But the girl burst out, "Here he is! Here is the boy who was our salvation! Here is our hero! We would all have been dead in the crick but for this here boy!"

Several other half-familiar people surged forward, pinning Mother to the wall. The men were not so outgoing as the girls, but all were very loud with their gratitude. I could hardly draw breath from the number of wet kisses and claps on the back I was receiving.

I looked up once to see Lucille gazing down from the

stairway in blank amazement. Then she shifted her gaze to Lowell who was behind me and a new look came into her eyes.

Above the din, Mother's voice howled out, "What are these people doing in my house?"

ꙮ 14 ꙮ

UNSEEN HAND GUIDES YOUTHFUL HERO
by Lowell Seaforth of the PANTAGRAPH staff
See related story: AWFUL CONFLAGRATION CLAIMS
CRAZED PERPETRATOR

*Alexander Armsworth, Horace Mann schoolboy
of Pine Street, stepped out of the Saturday night
darkness to alert Motorman G. V. Rafferty of im-
pending trouble on the Snake Creek trestle. The
half-filled trolley making its late run was thus
halted short of the bridge, dangerously weakened
by axe and flame. (See Amory Timmons obituary
on last page.)*

*The modest rescuer of nearly a score of lives
vanished from the hellish creekside but not before
he was identified. A deputation of survivors led by
Motorman Rafferty called at the Armsworth home
yesterday only to find that young Alexander's
family, the prominent Joe Armsworths and their*

debutante daughter, were unaware of their young hero's timely exploit.

Closely questioned, the plucky lad revealed that the ghost of a young girl who in a former incarnation had evidently been lost in a similar disaster, appeared to him with a warning. Interpreting this spectral message delivered in the Armsworth barn-loft, the boy acted with speed, flagging the trolley in his nightshirt. (See related story: Local Clergy Disturbed by News of Spiritualism.)

Crowds of the curious have already begun their pilgrimage to the Ghost Barn. Mrs. Joe Armsworth begs to inform the public that she is not at home to anyone and that trespassers will be prosecuted. The St. Louis papers are interested.

Crowds of the curious milled around down at the end of the lane from early Monday on. I was at home to observe them in the distance since Mother said I was to skip school until this blew over. Dad mentioned that as anything unusual is in short supply, this was not likely to blow over anytime soon. Lucille was in an agitated state, eying me with unspoken suspicions. She was still not sure whether she and Tom had been spoofed or spooked. And either way, she didn't like the attention I was getting.

Neither did I. Mother drew the blinds early Monday and gave me a good grilling. She was unable to swallow this ghost business, and unwilling. I wasn't allowed farther than the front porch and then only as Dad was making an early start to work.

"Well, Alexander," Dad said, "I had hoped that once Lucille's party was out of the way, we could settle back to some normal living. Now my hopes are dashed." He rummaged around for his cigar clipper and continued, "But this new development is your story, and you are stuck with it."

"Dad," I said, "to the best of my knowledge it is all true."

"Alexander," he said, "if I didn't think that, you would already be skinned and hung up to dry. The thing about it is, you were not cut out for a quiet life because you are honest to a fault. As your mother is not within hearing, I'll say to you that you are a throwback to Uncle Miles, God help you." Then he nipped off his cigar end and started down the porch steps into his day.

By afternoon, the sheriff had posted a guard at the end of the lane. Still, Cousin Elvera Schumate got through. She advanced toward the house, and there was no bird on her hat. She was strictly business.

"Luella," she said, "I have come to you in your hour of need."

"Oh, Elvera," Mother said, "if it is not one thing, it is another. I believe in my heart we are cursed. First Tom Hackett and now this. Vulgar publicity will finish off our good name. I don't know why I even try. It has all been for my children, and it seems they are both out to ruin us all they can." She spoke at length on this theme and fingered her cameo.

Cousin Elvera said, "There, there, do not take on."

And Mother replied, "You don't know what it is, Elvera. A childless woman cannot know the grief."

Gladys came into the parlor more than once to say that quite a number of people wanted to talk to me over the telephone. She'd chatted with them all. One was a reporter from the Alton paper who would pay to see the barn. One was somebody local who claimed to be a ghost catcher. And one was a lady from Pittsfield who had regular conversations with the dead and would be glad to team up with me. Mother told Gladys to hang up without conversing henceforth.

It was a well-nigh endless day, particularly after Cousin Elvera got there. She and Mother spent the afternoon murmuring in the parlor. I had not thought I was one to mind missing school, but I took to roaming without purpose around the house and staring up at the ceilings, thinking that if I could perceive an Inez, Captain Campbell might be the next step.

Lucille finally came in from the high school and exploded all over the parlor. She was in a temper since none of her friends wanted to speak of her party but persisted in quizzing her about my fame. Mother replied that the less said of both events, the better. Lucille went to her room.

Then Mother called me into the parlor, and I could see her powwow with Cousin Elvera had come to a satisfactory conclusion. "Alexander, draw near and sit down on that horsehair sofa. There are times, Alexander, when it is better to be thought a naughty, untruthful boy than—than to be thought an eccentric one. Do you follow me?"

I did not and said so.

"Let me try it another way," Mother said, shooting a glance at Cousin Elvera, who nodded. "It was a very brave thing to have hailed that streetcar and saved all those people. And they are all very grateful, as you know. Do you follow me?"

I did and said so, but I was not so much as a word ahead of her.

"Well then, it would be better not to take any credit whatever for doing a good deed, as might have been in your mind when you stole away from the scene of the —accident Saturday night. But when people come to you with hearts full of gratitude, you have to acknowledge it and you have a right to. Are you still attending me?"

I was and said so, and fairly interested since Mother had never before informed me of any of my rights.

"And so, we—I do not see why you must hide your light under a bushel and—and share your credit with—somebody else. You have my permission to announce to all and sundry that you were only acting on a hunch—

or perhaps something Bub might have told you. That your story about the—barn was only a fabrication. And then you need not share your glory with a—a—"

"Ghost," said Cousin Elvera, "particularly since there is no such thing."

It was my private opinion that if they had displayed ghosts down at the St. Louis World's Fair, she would be quick enough to claim she had shaken all their hands personally.

I didn't like the idea of retracting my first story, especially since it was true. On the other hand, I didn't like defying Mother and Cousin Elvera whose combined forces could stop the U.S. Cavalry cold. I told Mother I would give her words serious thought and headed to my room without making any commitments.

On my way upstairs, I heard Cousin Elvera say, "He is a sensible boy basically, and I feel sure he will come around to our way of thinking."

"If he was a sensible boy," Mother said, "we would not be in this mess."

I sat up on my windowsill gazing without thought down on the barn that afternoon. Suddenly, the barn door opened a crack. Then it was ajar, and Blossom Culp's head appeared from inside, turning to scan the yard. She seemed to signal an all-clear to someone behind her. Then she crept out into the lane. Following her was a man carrying a tripod camera and a device for flash powder.

She put her finger to her lips and then pointed down

to the gravel. The two of them made a silent retreat toward the side of the barn. Before they disappeared, though, she halted the stranger and put out her hand. He propped his tripod against the barn and dug into a pocket, coming up with folding money. Blossom deposited it down her shirtwaist front, and the two of them departed.

That night Cousin Elvera stayed to supper, and the conversation touched on every topic except recent issues. I was up in my room again by nine. I knew Mother expected me to make an early retraction of my story, and I was half persuaded to go along with her. A quiet night would have convinced me. But that's not the way matters arranged themselves.

I slept for a while and awoke to moonlight. Slipping over to the window, I surveyed the barn. But if Inez was afoot that night, she was sending no signals. One more trip to the barn, I thought, and I will put the whole business out of my mind and be quit of it. I drifted down through the creaking house and out across the yard.

With any luck, I said to myself, Blossom will not be charging admission at this hour. I thought this notion was somewhat witty, but my heart was in my mouth anyway.

As a rule, a murky flight of stairs is not comforting. But the darker and quieter, the better, I thought. When I pushed the door open, a strong smell of swamp water came from above. I slipped in and stood to one side of the moonlight. It picked up the girl's footprint, which was black and glistening wet. I tried not to concentrate on that, but the rest of the place was in shadow.

There was a whimpering then, and I nearly took flight. I blinked my eyes and thought I saw Trixie's bedraggled little dogface, but it was suspended above the floor in a corner. By degrees I could see the dog clearer and that she was being held. A white hand smoothed her tangled fur.

"Inez?" I said, not loud. "It's me."

"There are many intruders," her voice came back, "but I know you are the boy from the house." It was her same voice with the strange accent. But she was not agitated.

"Have they told you I do not exist?" she said, going right to the heart of the matter.

"They don't want you to exist, I guess."

"The living wish to forget the dead," she sighed. She was in a very different frame of mind. "But it does not matter. You saved the people in the train, all but the madman."

It wasn't a question, but I told her I did, thanks to her.

"Even the madman rests easier than I," she said, sighing again. Trixie whimpered. "I had thought to be saved, but my rescuer was my robber. I am even denied a decent grave."

"Why are you here, Inez?" I whispered.

"Because of that."

"Are you a soul in torment, Inez?"

"Yes," she said, "though there are quiet times. In my loneliness I have watched you from the window."

I did not like the thought of that but said nothing.

"I have watched you since you were old enough to walk, and I have looked out across the fields before the town was here."

"Then you are old, Inez."

"No, I am not old. I was spared that."

"What do you want?" I asked her as most of my fear left me.

"To be among my own people. Like me, they are above the ground, but they rest."

"How can I help?"

"There is little you can do alone," she said. "For a boy is hard to believe."

"Then why do you appear to me?"

"I have no choice among those who will see me and those who will not, and little experience of either."

"Blossom's Mama says I'm receptive."

"There are many ways to express it."

"But you appeared to Lucille too and to Tom Hackett."

"She was in danger—or he was. Perhaps I could do it because she was your sister. Besides, they were intruders here."

"I wish I could help you, Inez."

"Perhaps you can if you find me," she said. "But you will need the help of other believers—true believers."

"But aren't you here?"

"I am not here, but near. You will know me if you find me."

"How?"

For an answer, the shadows moved, and Inez stepped onto the moonlit floor. Her skirts covered the wet footprint, and Trixie was all but lost in the folds of her skirt. Inez seemed to stare through the floor, her face in shadow. But she pointed to the brooch that held her old-fashioned collar together. The moonlight caught its tiny flowers beneath the glass oval.

"This is all he left me," she said in a very ghostly voice this time. "And this is how you will know me."

Then she was gone, and I was staring at the footprint in the empty loft. But I heard her voice once more and never again: *"Not here, but near."*

❧ 15 ❧

I WAS IN MY SCHOOL KNICKERS AND SIT-
ting to a family breakfast of scrapple and bacon when
Cousin Elvera began her pounding on our front door
next morning. Mother had decided I was to go to school
if only to spread the word among my chums that I'd
been lying about Inez. Remembering how Blossom had
once fared at the hands of our classmates, I had no in-
tention of doing this. Still, I was glad not to be under
house arrest. The words of Inez were strong in my mind
but hard to decipher.

"Look at this!" Cousin Elvera said, rocketing into the
dining room. "It is the St. Louis *Democrat*, and your
name will be a byword of ridicule nationwide!"

Mother clutched her cameo, and Dad said, "Elvera,
take a chair." She was beside herself but enjoying it.
Her corsets squeaked in time to her breathing. She began to read aloud. The article covered the same ground
as Lowell's, but it embroidered considerably, calling

Inez a "fearful apparition" and me "a shyly sensitive and mystical lad, given to swooning and introspection."

"I can see you did not grant this interview, Alexander," Dad said. "What a lot of balderdash, Elvera."

"You don't know the worst, Joe," she replied, holding up the St. Louis *Democrat*. Taking up half a page was a photo of our barnloft, though not a clear picture. The wet footprint was only a smudge on the floor. The central feature was Mother's dress form. When she recognized herself, so to speak, she fell back in her chair. The headline over the photograph read:

Spectral Barn Where Dread Visitor Foretells Future Horrors

"Horrors," said Mother, "we are standing on the abyss. You won't be attending school again today, Alexander."

"I guess we ought to have a guard posted at the back of the property too," remarked Dad.

"If you ask me, Joe," Cousin Elvera said, "that is a classic example of shutting the barn door after the cat is out of the bag." She smiled, very satisfied at this clever statement, and added, "People will be carting away souvenirs next."

"Or that nasty little arachnid, that Blossom, who Alexander is sweet on, will start selling the bricks off the barn. She is of the class to take liberties," Lucille said.

I said nothing.

"I wish you would all be quiet. You too, Alexander," Mother said, very near tears. "You are all as bad as the public, and no one knows the pain I am being put to." She flung herself out of her chair and swept over to the bay window to stare out through a Boston fern. "I think," she said in slow and tragic tones, "we had just as well sell the house and— Dear Lord, an automobile has gotten through the barrier and is coming up the lane. What good is it to have a guard posted? We are as vulnerable here as early settlers!"

Dad joined her at the window and said, "It's a Cadillac."

"What does that matter—a Cadillac, you say?"

"Yes," said Dad, "and there is only one in town."

"Mrs. Van Deeter!" Mother and Cousin Elvera shrieked in unison. I continued with my scrapple and bacon, though the noise was very nearly unbearable.

Mother stood poised between the door to the front hall and the other one to the kitchen. She clearly didn't know whether to take courage or to take flight. A gentle knocking came at the front door. "It is surely only their chauffeur," Mother said, "but what can he want?"

"We could all go down the cellar and hide out in the coal bin until he's gone," Dad remarked to goad her on. Mother set off toward the front door, and the rest of us were not far behind. It's not every day when the richest and most invisible people in six counties send their automobile around.

Mother fumbled the door open, and there stood a lady. While not young, she was unusually beautiful. Warm though the morning was, she had a few fur skins draped around her shoulders, along with a big bunch of fresh violets. She was just turning the veil back over her hat, and there were a couple of rings on her fingers that could have served as Cadillac headlamps.

"Why, Mrs. Van Deeter, how do you do, I'm sure," Mother said. "This is an unexpected pleasure. I do hope you were put to no trouble in getting past the guard."

"None whatever," Mrs. Van Deeter said, smiling firmly. "I hope you will permit a call at this unseemly hour. I have been remiss in my social obligations and am endeavoring to do better."

Mother recovered slowly. "May I present my—" She looked around to find us all there. "My—entire family." She managed to introduce us all, though she was somewhat vague as to our names. Then Mrs. Van Deeter was shown into the parlor, and we all settled in around her. A silence followed while she arranged her fur skins.

"It is very nice to find you all in," she said at length. "Quite like a family party.

"I was so sorry to have missed *your* party, Miss Armsworth," she said, suddenly remembering it, "and one reason for this call is to meet you. I read the sweet account of your debut in the *Pantagraph*."

Lucille gave her an uncertain smile, but the cat had her tongue.

Mother sent me out to Gladys for a pot of coffee, so I missed the next part of the visit. I was hard put to convince Gladys we had a live Van Deeter in the parlor. But when she was persuaded, she took down the silver pot and the thin china. While I was bearing this away, I said, "And I guess you better go out and offer the chauffeur some coffee too since we are evidently moving in the limousine circle now." Gladys said that this was truly the age of miracles.

When I came back to the parlor, no one had budged. Dad seemed to forget he had work to go to, and no one told Lucille she was already late for school. Mrs. Van Deeter had them all under her spell. She marked my entry with some interest. "I suppose," she said, "that I should confess the major impulse for my visit." Coffee spoons stopped stirring all around the parlor. "I am a reader of the St. Louis *Democrat*."

Mother drooped, saying, "Then I suppose you must have a dreadful impression of us, Mrs. Van Deeter. I could not blame you if you condemn us for the worst kind of publicity-seeking."

"Not at all," Mrs. Van Deeter said, smiling into her coffee cup. "On the contrary, I think this is the most interesting thing to have occurred in Bluff City in ages. It comes in good time. I for one had nearly expired of monotony. And I wonder if you might persuade Alexander to show me his Ghost Barn."

"Oh, Alexander, see how low you have brought us!"

Mother accused me. Then her face changed, and she said, "You say you would care to see the barn, Mrs. Van Deeter?"

"I yearn to," she replied calmly.

Mother and Cousin Elvera leaned toward one another to converse in low tones. But Mrs. Van Deeter said with a little frost on her voice, "Have you ladies considered just what a social asset a bit of novelty is in a small town?" Their heads parted, and they gaped at her.

"Well, Alexander," Dad said, "as you're the hero of the hour, you better lead the way." Everybody stood up, but Mrs. Van Deeter said, "Oh, won't you permit Alexander to conduct me on a private tour?"

"I never go there myself," Mother said, sinking back on the sofa. "I'm afraid you will find the place terribly dusty."

"It will only add to the effect," Mrs. Van Deeter said as she took me by the arm.

I was getting fairly experienced at leading ladies around. But I wondered if Mrs. Van Deeter was merely making sport of me, and I knew if I did not show her a good time, Mother would take it out of my hide.

We were approaching the barn when Mrs. Van Deeter said, "Tell me about your ghost girl, Alexander. Do you see her with regularity?"

"Only twice to speak to," I said.

"What is she like?"

"Well, her name is Inez Dumaine. She has a small damp dog with a sore leg. And the first time I saw her she said the dead are robbed and cannot forestall it. And she said, 'My hoops, my hoops,' or words to that effect."

"Women once wore hoop skirts," Mrs. Van Deeter mused. "Long ago, of course. And then she warned you about the burning trestle?"

"In so many words. She did not make herself too plain."

"I see. And she appeared again?"

"Last night," I said, "but I haven't made any mention of that."

"Did she issue further warnings?"

"No, she spoke of her own concerns, which were harder to figure. She said she wanted to be with her own people who are above the ground but resting. Then she showed me her brooch and said she was near but not here. That there is a hitching post with her initials," I pointed out.

"How intriguing."

We entered the barn, and Mrs. Van Deeter gathered her skirts to climb the stairs. Grand though she is, she's quite game. "That's our Mercer," I mentioned in passing.

"I'm afraid I don't know one auto from another. I take it this is quite a good one?"

I told her it was.

Upstairs, she pronounced the whole loft "eerie in the extreme." She examined everything and stooped to touch the wet footprint. She remarked upon the swampy smell, and I said that Inez had evidently died in water. Mrs. Van Deeter thought that was sad and looked it.

On our way back to the house, she gave my arm a squeeze and said she had been quite frightened the whole time, though she had not shown it. "I think," she said as we came back into the parlor, "that as you are so brave, I will call you Alexander the Great."

Lucille pulled an ugly face when she heard that, but broke into a winning smile when Mrs. Van Deeter glanced at her. Cousin Elvera and Mother were sitting close and looking like outlaws awaiting a verdict. But Dad said, "Well, Mrs. Van Deeter, what do you make of it all? Are you a believer?"

"I am now. I think it quite remarkable and quite mysterious—and my guide was charming." She was persuaded to take another cup of coffee and engaged Dad in a discussion about autos. She said her husband found the Cadillac a bit confining, and she thought he might prefer a Mercer for his own use. Triumph was beginning to spread across Mother's face. She beamed at me particularly. Cousin Elvera smiled and nodded as if Mercers and ghosts were a couple of things she was especially partial to.

Then the front door banged back, and Uncle Miles stalked into the parlor in his overalls. "WHAT IN THE DAMMIT TO HELL IS THERE A COP IN THE LANE FOR?" he roared.

"Lost," Mother murmured behind her handkerchief. "All is lost."

❧ 16 ❧

SINCE HE'D CAUGHT US WITH OUR GUARD down, Uncle Miles raved on at some length: "I was up at Whitehall a couple of days to the steam engine rally. And what do I find when I get back? The whole damn town runnin' wild! The trestle down and a trolley with it. Amory Timmons dead! The *Pantagraph* full of Alexander here. Your lane blocked off by the law, Joe! And—WELL DAMN ME TO HELL, HOW'D THEY GET YOU HERE, MRS. VAN DEETER?" Uncle Miles blinked behind his spectacles at her sitting there in the best chair.

"Oh, I came of my own accord, Miles. I had to see for myself the source of all the excitement—just like you."

"Well, Luella," he said, turning to Mother, "This is a great day for you, ain't it? It'd take unearthly forces to get Van Deeters through your doors!"

"Now, Miles," said Mrs. Van Deeter mildly, "don't tease."

"Ah—Uncle Miles," Dad began.

"I know, Joe, I know. I am the bull in the china shop and always was. But if somebody will just tell me what all the fuss is about, I'll be gone. You know I never rest till I know everything. It keeps me modern."

In a far-off voice, Mother said to Mrs. Van Deeter, "You know my husband's uncle?"

"To be sure. He does all my cabinet-making. I would be lost without him."

"*That's* the truth," Uncle Miles agreed, "but let's us get back to this present business. Alexander, the way I hear it, everything stems from you."

There is nothing to be done with Uncle Miles but to give things to him straight, so I did. I told him everything except about seeing Inez again the night before. He heard me out with his hands on his hips, glaring somewhat.

"So that's it, is it?" he said, not showing any astonishment. "Things will out."

"I just want it over and done with," Mother sighed.

"Enjoy it while you may, Luella. You're not liable to get this much attention again. However, if you do want it all put behind you, you're goin' about it all the wrong way as usual."

Mrs. Van Deeter smiled and asked what the right way might be.

"Easy," said Uncle Miles. "Drawin' out a mystery only inflames people's imaginations. Let everybody in to have their look, same as Mrs. Van Deeter here. People like a satisfactory conclusion all tied up neat. And then we got to lay the ghost of Inez Dumaine. Nobody told me she was stalkin' abroad! Nobody tells me nothin' but rumor and nonsense!"

"Hold on a minute, Uncle Miles," said Dad. "Do you mean that you believe—"

"Hold on to yourself, Joe. I'm not finished. If this whole business is allowed to drag out, people will flock to Alexander, expectin' him to tell their fortunes and read their palms and find missin' articles and I don't know what. It could go on for years. How'd you like *that*, Luella?"

Mother wouldn't like that at all, as was evident from her face.

Then Uncle Miles turned to Dad and said, "I have knowed about Inez Dumaine for better than fifty years. I didn't know she was not restin' easy, but I should have figured she wouldn't since stands to reason. And yes, Joe, there is such a thing as restless spirits, and whether mortals believe in them or not hasn't got any bearin' on the situation. Any fool knows that, even this boy here."

"I believe you have a story to tell us, Miles," said Mrs. Van Deeter. "Perhaps you would be more comfortable if you took a chair."

"I don't mind if I do," said Uncle Miles, "but I chew when I talk." He pulled a plug out of his overalls and gnawed it down to size. "And it wouldn't be a bad thing to have somebody from the *Pantagraph* to come over and take notes on the history of this affair. Go ahead and have somebody sent for. I'm in no hurry."

It was a quarter of an hour before Lowell, who was sent for, arrived. Mrs. Van Deeter stayed rooted to her chair, calming Mother considerably by mentioning that now they were acquainted she looked forward to entertaining us Armsworths at her house one day, invitation to include Cousin Elvera. Though mollified by this, Mother was still a bundle of nerves. She went out to the kitchen once and cleared her head by screaming at Gladys.

Lowell walked in, took one look at Uncle Miles, and flipped his notebook open. He gave Lucille several glances before things got started, and she returned them all.

Uncle Miles gargled his throat clear, "It was either eighteen-hundred and sixty-one or sixty-two. I don't recall which, and it don't matter. At any rate it was just before the war got goin' good. I was not more than thirty-five, but too old for soldierin'. Otherwise I would very likely not be here today.

"There was considerable new money here in town then as now." He shot a look at Mother. "So I was busy with carpentry. I had my own shed for storin' lumber, which I worked out of.

"One day a fellow I had never laid eyes on come into the shed and said he'd heard I was the man to see if you wanted to get a gang of workmen together to put up a house. I told him he was not mistaken.

"He was a fellow in his middle years and said his

name was Captain Campbell. He had a military bearin', and I would have took him for a cavalry officer if he had not been so stout.

"He said he had ready money and wanted the best house it would build. He had bought an acre out in the country, which is right where we sit now, of course, as I'm tellin' you this.

"Well, sir, he engaged me to do his contractin', and we laid out the terms. 'Are you a family man?' I says to him. 'No,' says he, 'why do you ask?' 'Well,' I says, 'if a woman is to live in the house, she'll have notions as to how it is to be fitted out.' 'No,' he says, 'I am alone, but it has always been my dream to have a grand big house on dry land.' I thought that was a peculiar way of puttin' it, but I did not say anythin'.

"I showed him several styles of houses from my book of plans. But nothin' suited. The next day he came back with a drawin' he had made hisself. When I seen it, I said, 'Them porches you have sketched in are very like the covered decks on a steamboat.'

"He was silent for a minute and then said, "Well, it is not to be wondered at, for I have spent my life over on the Mississippi River at the wheel of various boats.' He didn't call the boats by name, and I didn't ask. Then he said, 'I would take it as a favor if these particulars of my life are not known in these parts.' I told him no one would hear anything from me, and have not broke my word till now.

"This fellow who called hisself Captain Campbell and

I struck up a friendship, in so far as he was friendly with anybody. We moved right along with the construction work because with the war breakin', we didn't know but what materials might be hard to come by.

"The marble for that mantel there come from Vermont, and all the other stonework come over from Indiana. The brick was locally fired, but he would have nothin' but the best despite his haste.

"The house was pretty near topped off when one time him and me was out here. It was evening, and he was showin' me just where he wanted the brick barn to be. He was inclined to be talkative and presently drew out a jar of blended whiskey. We passed it back and forth till near dark and began to talk of several things.

"I didn't think he had drunk to excess, but his voice took on a new sound, and he says, 'Miles, now that I see my house standin' up against the sky, I wonder what was in my mind to raise it. There is no end to man's folly, Miles, as I expect you know.'

"Of course I did know that, but I didn't say anythin'.

"'A man can want somethin' to the point of indecency,' he said, 'and when he attains his goal, it is ashes in his mouth and a bad conscience.'

"I told him that if he had things to reproach hisself with, he was no different from any other man. 'You do not know whereof you speak in my case, Miles,' he says. 'but I am too heavy-laden to carry my guilt unspoken any longer. I want your ear, Miles, and I want your silence.'

"I told him he had both, and he said, 'I have seen my life plain, and it is a fearsome spectacle.' Then he got to his story.

"He said his real name was Captain Thibodaux and that he had worked out of the port of New Orleans all his river days. With the war between the states pendin', New Orleans was in a state of panic. People of quality and substance was streamin' out of it and would pay any money for passage north. He had a boat comin' up to Keokuk, and once he'd booked the cabins, he booked the deck space too. Still, people come to him in herds.

"Well, it seemed he knowed a Creole family of New Orleans—the Dumaines. They was French speakers but wealthy and highly thought of. Mr. Dumaine come to him and said that though business was keeping hisself and wife in New Orleans, he wanted his daughter took north. He had grave doubts about the fate of the South and wanted his girl, Inez, safe with a family he knowed up at Galena.

"Captain Thibodaux couldn't deny a friend the safety of his daughter, and so he made room for her on the boat, takin' her aboard from the river side after dark to avoid the crowds. She was high-spirited and demanded they take her dog with her.

"Then this Captain Thibodaux told me the name of his boat. It was the *Plaquemine Belle*."

Uncle Miles halted his story and looked around at us. Lowell glanced up from his notebook. "Well, I can see I have outlived my time if nobody here remembers the *Plaquemine Belle*. It was famous enough in its day. On that last run I'm tellin' you about, one of its boilers sprang a leak off Grand Tower, and another one did the same when the boat was off St. Genevieve.

"Still, Captain Thibodaux pressed on, thinkin' if war was declared, all the Southern boats would be commandeered. And he wanted to be as far north as possible in hopes of escapin' notice. He knowed it was a long shot and that he was playin' with the lives of all concerned. But he ordered the boat on as fast as she would go under the circumstances.

"Well, both boilers went finally, just twelve miles west of here in midstream. Captain Thibodaux was blowed clear, bein' on deck. So he didn't have the option of goin' down with his ship. The river was full of bodies and burnin' debris. He thrashed around in the water, not knowin' how to strike for land as it was night.

"Presently, Inez Dumaine floated up, clingin' to a scrap of the deck. She was heavy as lead, to hear him tell it. But he got her up on the lumber where her little dog was challengin' all comers. Somehow the captain got himself across the raft too, and they was but barely afloat for some hours.

"They come to shore just before daybreak, and with that, Captain Thibodaux recovered his senses and seen his act of folly had cost him the lives of any number of passengers, his good name, and the *Plaquemine Belle*.

"He helped Inez Dumaine onto a sandbar. She took one step on land and then fell down exhausted. The only solace to the captain's conscience was that he'd saved her who was in his special care. Then he turned Inez over and seen she was dead. He wept when he told me."

Mrs. Van Deeter gripped the arms of her chair and leaned forward. Uncle Miles paused and ran his hand over his brow. He used a brass bowl for a spittoon and went on. "Such passengers as had escaped fire and water had fetched up on the far shore, in Missouri. Captain Thibodaux figured they would count him among the dead. And he thought it was just as well.

"He was half-crazed when he looked on Inez's dead face. His first notion was that he didn't want to bury her on a sandbar. She was a carefully reared girl who had been educated by the French nuns. So, he picked her up and began to walk inland with her. It was in his mind to find her a Christian graveyard.

"The dog followed as best it could over the rough ground. It was a lap dog, of course, half-drowned, and had broke its leg. The captain was in a bad state hisself and had to put down Inez's body periodically to rest. The sun dried her skirts, but still she was a heavy burden. Once when the captain stopped to rest, he seen that around the hoops in her skirts there were weighty bundles sewed in. He tore open the hem of her skirt, and a diamond bracelet spilled out.

"He ripped at the rest of her hoops, and bit by bit out dropped the Dumaine family fortune in the form of jewels sewed into Inez's skirts for safe passage north.

"Well," Uncle Miles said, "there set a man in a field with his reputation and his livelihood lost to him and a fortune in his hands. He was overcome by temptation, and who's spotless enough to condemn him?

"The thought of givin' Inez a Christian burial give way in his mind to hidin' her body and startin' anew with her wealth. It was wrong, but that's the way it was. He carried her on across the country, which was thinly settled in those days. And when he could go no farther, he was at the edge of Bluff City, and it was night. He left her body in a pasture and went to steal a spade from a farm nearby. When he came back, her dog that had followed her to the last was dead on her breast.

"He buried the girl and her dog and concealed the grave with brush. Then he stole away in the night. But when he'd converted the jewelry to cash somewheres and had disguised hisself with chin whiskers, he come back to Bluff City.

"He went to the farmer who owned the pasture where Inez was and bought an acre of it for spot cash. And that was where he raised his house. 'After all,' he said to me, 'it was her money and if I couldn't let her lay in a Christian's grave, I could at least have her by me. And then I didn't want anybody unearthin' her by chance.'

"He told me again just exactly where to have the

bricklayers build his barn. Then he took me by the arm and led me to a spot nearby. There was a smooth stone sunk in the weeds there. 'Miles,' he said, 'that's where she lays. I don't dare to raise a proper headstone for her. But I want you to contract for a fine hitchin' post. And I want you to have her initials carved in it. That is as much as I can do for her.' "

The parlor was dead silent as Uncle Miles sat back in his chair. When no one spoke, he said, "Well, you know where the story went from there. Captain Campbell, as he called hisself, never spoke to me again on the matter. The barn went up and the hitchin' post beside it, which I had a gravestone cutter make. And in a month, they found the captain hangin' from the ceilin' in his house with a stepladder kicked out from under him. It was in this parlor."

Lucille whimpered.

❦ 17 ❧

LOWELL'S ARTICLE ON THE TRUE HIS-
tory of Inez Dumaine and Captain Thibodaux ran in
the *Pantagraph* next morning. Mother was half-recon-
ciled to all the publicity and had the sheriff call off the
guard on our lane. She still did not like Uncle Miles's
story and could not forgive me for stirring it up. But
then she had to admit it was Inez Dumaine who had
brought Mrs. Van Deeter to our door.

The town turned out for Amory Timmons's funeral.
Dad was a pallbearer, and I sat with Bub and his ma on
mourners' row. There was a procession out to the
cemetery, swelled by curious strangers who read the
Pantagraph.

Dad took the Mercer, and once Amory was buried,
we were ready to leave in haste since people were point-
ing me out. Dad was just putting his foot out on the
runningboard to ease the accelerator down when Mother
said, "Step on it, Joe. Here comes Uncle Miles."

He was striding between the headstones in his rusty blue suit and a celluloid collar but no tie. Dad called out, "Want a ride back to town, Uncle Miles?"

"Hell no, Joe. I don't ride in them things. They ain't dignified. But say listen, now we got Amory settled, it's time to see to Inez Dumaine. It won't do to put that off."

"Oh, Uncle Miles, I don't know what you mean," Mother said through her veil. "Talk like that isn't right on poor Amory's funeral day."

"Luella, I will be underground myself directly," he replied, "so let's us have less of your lecturing on the subject."

"Well, just what is it you have in mind, Uncle Miles?" Dad asked.

"I wonder you cannot figure it for yourself, Joe. We have to dig up Inez from under the hitchin' post and get her buried with her own people."

"She said her people were above the ground but resting," I sang out before I thought.

"You haven't told this before, Alexander." Mother turned to give me a hard look where I was shrinking on the back seat. "Are you adding to your story to keep yourself in the center of attention?"

"Very likely," sniffed Lucille, who was on the back seat with me.

"Be that as it may," Uncle Miles went on, "there is sense to what Alexander says. Inez Dumaine's folks was New Orleans people. And down in New Orleans the dead are buried in marble vaults above ground on account of the swampy condition of the soil. You only have to stick your shovel in New Orleans ground to strike water. Which anybody would know who travels or takes an interest in the world."

"Did *you* know that?" Mother asked me.

I told her no.

"I do not see how this is any of our responsibility," she murmured to herself.

"Well, I have already made it plain to you, Luella," said Uncle Miles. "You won't rest until Inez does. People will be trampin' your property and doggin' you by day and night. If you don't take no pity on Inez, I reckon you'll take pity on yourself."

"We will have to think this out," Mother said lamely.

"Thinkin' ain't doin'," said Uncle Miles and stalked off among the gravestones.

When we turned in the lane at home, there was a woman sitting up on our piazza in the bentwood settee. And the nearer we got, the more familiar she was. "Oh who can that be?" Mother complained. "It seems we are holding an unending open house."

It was my teacher, Miss Winkler. As the Mercer drew up to the house, she rose, clutching her satchel, and gave us one of her small, wintery smiles. It was only a few days till the end of school, and I was one among several who would not mind being set free.

"Have you been acting up at school?" Mother hissed

at me. I reminded her I hadn't been to school all week. "Then that must be it," she said, stepping down out of the Mercer. I had to go along up to the porch to say how do you do to Miss Winkler. Mother said, "I hope you do not mind that we kept Alexander out these past days."

Miss Winkler replied that on the whole, she did not consider it had been a bad plan. Then I escaped, thinking it prudent to keep clear of them. They were on the porch for some time.

At supper, Mother said that the entire ghost situation had all but undone Miss Winkler's attempts to teach scientific methods and a modern outlook on things. According to her, the children were all restless and would talk of nothing but dreadful prophecies, destruction, and the living dead.

That had caused Mother to mention to her Uncle Miles's plan to open the grave. Miss Winkler replied that if it would put an end to the matter it was worth doing. She thought that the whole story was pure folklore anyway and that there'd be nothing found under the hitching post. She was inclined to bring along the whole class to show them their foolishness.

Mother took to the idea at once as it would discredit both Uncle Miles and Inez Dumaine in one stroke. So that was what finally sold her on allowing the grave to be opened.

A good while later, Blossom told me she'd come upon Miss Winkler nosing around outside the barn while we were still at Amory's funeral. Blossom tried to charge her fifty cents to be taken through the loft. But Miss Winkler got her down to a quarter.

It was on the last day of school that the grave of Inez Dumaine was opened. Long enough, according to Mother, to let things get completely out of hand again. It was shaping up to be the largest gathering ever held at our place, and Mother was torn between presiding over it and locking herself in her room. But like most things meant to settle a matter once and for all, it led instead to a whole new enterprise—for me and for Blossom Culp too.

Father Ludlow from the church made known his wish to be present in case the proceedings called for religion. Uncle Miles thought that was nonsensical. But Mother said a church representative would add some much-needed tone if the thing was to be done at all.

Every train that made a Bluff City stop brought another reporter from some out-of-town newspaper. They put up at the Abraham Lincoln Hotel and were seen rubbernecking around the square in yellow spats.

The betting was said to be heavy among them on the question of whether or not anything would be found under the hitching post. The St. Louis *Democrat* reporter wired back a story with this headline:

DUMAINE'S REMAINS OR BLUFF CITY BLUFF?
TOMORROW WILL TELL THE TALE

Jake McCulloch planned to attend too. He's the undertaker and offered to provide two gravediggers without charge. "That Jake is the sharpest advertiser in town," Dad mentioned. "See if he doesn't turn up in his new motorized hearse to show it off."

Cousin Elvera called on the telephone the evening before and asked Mother if they hadn't ought to wear black. She had mourning togs left over from Mr. Schumate's passing. Mother said that was the most grotesque thing she'd ever heard.

Cousin Elvera's voice crackled right out of the receiver, "Luella, you will be talking out of the other side of your mouth if Mrs. Van Deeter shows up in black. And are you thinking of serving punch? If you are, I am available for pouring as I want to support you in every way I can."

"No punch," Mother said and hung the receiver back on the wall.

I stood at my window that night, gazing out to the barn. But there was not a flicker of light, nor any sign there ever had been. It seemed likely that Inez knew what was coming, and already her restless soul was easier.

I reckoned that mine was too, though there was an empty place in me where Inez had lodged herself. If the whole matter was to be settled, people would forget in time. And I was not sure I wanted to be one of them. Maybe some unbeliever in the future could convince me none of it ever happened. The twentieth century did not look to be an age with any patience for the past. Ghosts were surely falling out of fashion just as fast as Captain Thibodaux's gingerbread porches or girls the size of Lucille.

These were my thoughts that night, alone up in my room, and finally I went to bed. But in a way I did see Inez one more time, looking the way I had known her. It was a dream, though more memorable than most.

Like all dreams, it began with a jumble. But then I saw a scene clear. There was a long marble box which was both a table and a tomb. And around it sat three people, having coffee in the out of doors.

Inez was at the head of the table in her swampy-green dress, pouring out a cup and offering it to Mrs. Van Deeter who was covered head to foot in black veils. Blossom Culp sat at the end with her black spider legs thrust up on the tomb top and crossed at the ankles. Behind them was a shadowy person, who I took to be Blossom's Mama, passing around a tray of cakes from Lucille's coming out. Numbers of these table-tombs stretched away to a level horizon.

I drew nearer, saying I guessed the place where they were was New Orleans. They all laughed at that, but no sound came. The breeze fluttered Mrs. Van Deeter's veils, and Inez pointed to her brooch. Blossom threw her head back and laughed hardest of all, which was peculiar since in real life she is somewhat sober.

But it was Inez who spoke in her soundless way, saying, no, no, mercy, no, they were not in New Orleans.

They were in China because a person would have to dig that far before he would come across Dumaine's remains. Then the three of them were overcome with more mirth until the breeze blew up into a wind that caused the tomb lids to scrape and the coffee cups to funnel off like autumn leaves. Then the sun was streaming in my bedroom window.

People were streaming into the yard too, and the buzz of their voices was rising with the sun. When I got down to the dining room, Dad was trying to finish his breakfast in peace. Mother and Lucille were staring out through the Boston fern. Drawn up in the lane beside the bay window was Jake McCulloch's new motorized hearse.

It had frosted glass side panels presided over by a couple of flat brass angels holding up a swag of metal drapery. On the front door Jake's message was lettered in gold:

J. MC CULLOCH
RESPECTFUL INTERMENTS
LADY ASSISTANTS
TELEPHONE 640 DAY OR NIGHT
WE NEVER REST

Mother was looking past the hearse and shaking her head. "All those reporters in those terrible neckties. They are true racetrack types. I blame Lowell Seaforth for drawing them here from every direction like flies."

But Lucille lit into her and would not hear a word against Lowell, who was himself in the yard, milling with the rest.

There were autos and buggies the whole length of the lane. And when Mother saw Nelly Melba dragging up Uncle Miles's rig, she said, "We had better go outdoors, or he will be in here. Besides, there comes Elvera. Thank heaven she is wearing her gray cotton. You stay where you are, Alexander, until you have had your breakfast. The less of you in these proceedings, the better."

But even after I had a good hot breakfast under my belt, I hadn't missed much. People wandered about, uncertain as to how much ceremony the occasion called for. Miss Winkler had brought the rest of my class, which added to the numbers and noise.

When I stepped off the back porch, I was greeted by a few jeers from my schoolmates who don't take kindly to one of their number being singled out for special attention, even by fate. I didn't spot Blossom with them, but I didn't look too hard. She was likely not far off, as she usually is.

Jake's gravediggers were resting on their spades. Father Ludlow advanced and retreated. Whether or not to call everybody to prayer over a hitching post was taxing his judgment.

Uncle Miles looked purposeful in his overalls and Sunday shirt. He'd been supervising the lifting of the hitching post and had it laid to one side. The stone pony's head with the iron ring in its mouth was flat against the grass. People came up to examine it, as there was nothing else to see. We might all be milling over the backyard yet if Mrs. Van Deeter's Cadillac had not rolled through the parting mob.

Her chauffeur handed her down, and she was wearing a large purple hat and a fresh bunch of violets. "My goodness," she remarked in the sudden silence. "Whatever is the delay?" With that, each gravedigger planted a foot on his spade and turned earth.

They dug until the sun was squarely overhead and had to climb out of the hole every so often to drink cool water in the shade of the barn. Such observers as had brought their lunch sat under the trees and ate. Miss Winkler tried to conduct class there. "And so you will see, boys and girls, that in the clear light of day, the old myths and mysteries concocted by— imaginative—persons are revealed as the fiction they invariably are." The class ate their sandwiches and took very little interest in either the rising mound of earth or Miss Winkler.

"All right, boys," Uncle Miles's voice rumbled out at the gravediggers, "start takin' it a little easy." A crowd, mostly reporters, pushed up nearer the mounds, leaving room only for Mrs. Van Deeter.

One of the diggers threw up half a spadeful of dirt almost at Mrs. Van Deeter's feet. Sharper-eyed than all the rest, she cried out, "Stop!" Then she pointed a gloved finger and said, "Examine that clod!"

Uncle Miles bent down and scooped up the damp clay. Something was stuck in it and glittered. He crumbled the dirt away, and his spectacles slipped down his sweaty nose as he studied the object, cupped out of general view.

Every eye was on him when he held the thing up. I'd never seen his hand tremble, but it was unsteady then. He raised it higher and higher, like Father Ludlow giving a benediction. The sun caught the little oval in his hand.

It was a brooch, the one that belonged to Inez, and the glass on it was smooth and unclouded. Beneath it were the little flowers fashioned out of human hair.

I squinted up at it there, held against the sky in Uncle Miles's gnarled old hand. And it was the same brooch I had seen by moonlight in the loft. The tears came to my eyes, possibly because of trying to look into the sun. I remembered Inez's words about the brooch, *This is all he left me. And this is how you will know me.*

One of the reporters yelled out, "Bingo!" And the rest of them scratched notes in their pads. Father Ludlow worked his way to the front circle and cried out, "The lost is found; let us pray!" But then G. K. Rafferty, the motorman, muscled forward and called out, "Keep a-diggin'!" There was a pounding of feet approaching across the gravel, which I took to be the class deserting Miss Winkler.

The soil was flying up in smaller clods now, and the gravediggers' heads were down level with the yard. There were sweat stains spreading on their shirts. The brooch was closed in Uncle Miles's fist, and he stared down into the pit as stern and unflinching as if he was looking into his own grave.

Then both the diggers stood up and thrust their spades aside. One of them called for a broom, and presently it was passed to them over the heads of the crowd. People climbed higher on the piles of dirt, holding their hats and bending double, trying to see past the laborers.

One of them dropped to his knees to scoop back the dirt while the other manned the broom. Then somebody above them gasped and pointed. I didn't mean to look but did. There was a flash of white beneath the broom, and bone by bone a skeletal hand lay bare, flush with the yellow clay.

"There she is," a voice came, and echoed back through the pushing crowd. When more of the dirt was cleaned away, the bones of the hand were seen to be resting on a small skull. It looked no bigger than a squirrel's, but I knew it was Trixie.

A reporter held a camera out over the pit and squeezed the bulb. Sunlight flooded the grave like a halo as the gravediggers stood back. Then I cut and ran.

⚛ 18 ⚛

WHEN I GOT AS FAR AS THE BACK STEP, wondering if I was sick or only sorry, a heavy hand fell on my shoulder. I was turned around to face an over-sized man staring down at me from a great height. How he had blended into the crowd I did not know. He wore a white linen suit, a string tie, and a large Panama hat. His face under it was the size and color of a sugar-cured ham.

"As you are makin' for the house," he said, "I take it you are the Armsworth boy." I nodded at that. "I can see you are in haste, and I can divine why," he said. His straw hat bobbed in agreement. "To look upon the bare bones of a sweet soul with whom you have evidently communicated not many days past is a natural shock, hardly an experience suitable to be shared with curious strangers."

That was a good way of putting it, coming though

it did from one of the curious strangers. "I am from a part of the world where such experiences as yours are treated with more understandin'. Permit me to introduce myself—Mortimer Brulatour of New Orleans. I confess I too am a newspaper man, but trust I possess finer sensitivities than my Northern brethren.

"I am as keen after a story as any of them, but am up here on an errand of compassion besides." He leaned nearer and looked confidential. "It is my plan to personally accompany the bones—remains of Mademoiselle Dumaine back to the New Orleans cemetery of her ancestors and forebears.

"As this expedition is financed by my newspaper, I am compelled to find in the somber journey a story to be featured by the New Orleans *Delta Daily*.

"Though there is a lively interest in the spirit world down home, stories like this one do not crop up two for a penny. And so I will be in your debt if you will grant me an exclusive interview. I am prepared to make it worth your while as I have already laid out a sum of money to one of your little neighbor girls to be given an exclusive tour through the barn. Are the pair of you in cahoots?"

I was marveling at the honeyed tongue of this Brulatour fellow when suddenly a rumbling from the direction of Jake's hearse caused him to jerk around and narrow his eyes.

Brulatour made off around the corner of the house,

and I followed. The back doors of the hearse were standing open, and Jake was pulling out a polished-wood box. It was not as large as a coffin or the shape of one. It appeared to be a somewhat superior-type packing crate, fitted up with bronze handles. Jake had all he could do to manage it by himself as he staggered past us.

"One moment, my good man!" Mortimer Brulatour said, and Jake replied that he had no time because he had to collect the deceased. "When you have done so," Brulatour said, "kindly deliver her without delay to the depot, since I will be catching the 4:30 train."

Jake thumped his burden down on the grass and turned to confront the stranger. Though Jake has a farmer's face, his hands are as white and smooth as milk. He planted these hands on his hips and said grimly, "I don't know as we have met."

"Mortimer Brulatour of the New Orleans *Delta Daily*. I have undertaken to accompany the body south."

"I do the undertaking here," said Jake, "and you do not figure anywhere in my plans."

"Now see here," Brulatour replied on a rising note, "the city of Miss Dumaine's birth has some claims upon her, and as a representative of that city, I—"

"You are off your turf now, mister. The body will lie in my funeral parlor for as many days as I see fit so that the public can come and pay their respects. A good many people have not turned out today, thinking there would be nothing to it. But they'll have their chance to mourn the departed in my first-class establishment. The lid will be shut, of course, but I plan some floral offerings and organ music. You go about your business, and I'll go about mine."

Their voices carried across the yard. Several people who had stared their fill at the grave drifted over in search of fresh diversion. They made another circle around Jake and Brulatour, who looked to be squaring off for a fight.

Brulatour's face was shading to purple. "I have no doubt that such a public display would benefit your business no end. However, I have a deadline to comply with and can't accommodate you."

Jake took a step closer. "You can accommodate me and yourself by being on the 4:30 train. And I will ship the deceased at a later date in my own good time."

"I will have justice," Brulatour bawled, "even in this godforsaken crossroads village and—"

"WHO IN THE DAMMIT TO HELL IS SQUABBLIN' OVER THAT GIRL'S BONES LIKE A PAIR OF STARVED COYOTES?" Uncle Miles pushed his way up to the front of the crowd and glared.

"Now what?" Brulatour asked, exasperated. "Who is *this* rustic?"

Uncle Miles ignored him and turned on Jake. 'Listen, McCulloch, that little gal was robbed of her fortune by Thibodaux fifty years ago. I'm here to see you don't rob her of her dignity now. This here is one time you don't cash in on the dead." Jake glanced nervously around at the gathering crowd of future clients and looked mortified.

"Quite right," said Brulatour. "My sentiments exac—"

"And as for you," Uncle Miles jerked around, "*you* got no stake in the matter whatsoever." He smacked his eighty-five-year-old hands together like he might stretch Brulatour out on the lawn.

"You see this boy here?" he said, jabbing a finger toward me. "Me and him is the Alpha and Omega of this whole business. I raised that hitchin' post over Inez Dumaine in 1861 and this boy communed with her spirit here lately. If anybody is going to see her safely to her restin' place, it'll be him and me, which is what we're goin' to do."

And which is what we did, though I had not foreseen the possibility of making a trip to New Orleans with Uncle Miles, and I doubt if he'd thought of it before that moment himself. In the midst of the listening throng, I saw Blossom Culp watching, her eyes as black as ebony and both ears cocked.

"Out of the question!" Mother said from the sidelines. She'd stepped up in time to hear Uncle Miles's closing remarks. "Alexander will not be accompanying you to New Orleans or any other place, Uncle Miles. What a harebrained idea!"

"Surely it is time the boy saw something of the

world." The voice came from someone standing just behind Mother.

"I never heard such a crazy notion," Mother said, turning to see the speaker was Mrs. Van Deeter. "Oh, do you really think so? Perhaps you're right."

That's how Uncle Miles and I happened to be down at the depot that very day to catch the 4:30 train. Jake McCulloch washed his hands of the whole affair. So the box containing the bones of Inez and Trixie rode on the seat beside the Van Deeters' chauffeur. Mrs. Van Deeter shared the back seat of the Cadillac with Mother, who was glad enough to be seen driving all the way across town in such style and company. Dad took me in the Mercer, and Lucille and Lowell were on the back seat together.

Lowell was still covering the story, but every time I glimpsed behind, he and Lucille were sitting closer. And whispering. It was somewhat disgusting but a big improvement over Tom Hackett.

"You are to pay your own way on this trip, Alexander," Dad explained to me. He'd given me two ten-dollar bills to pin into my underwear and a pocketful of change. "And keep your eye on Uncle Miles. Since he won't act his age, you'll have to be grown-up enough for two."

❧ 19 ❧

UNCLE MILES SAT UPRIGHT IN THE DAY coach, and I sat across from him, looking out at the bean fields and black earth that gave way to the rocky yellow land of the southern part of the state.

When the conductor came through to look at our tickets, he told us we'd have to change at Carbondale for the Illinois Central's *Panama Limited*. Uncle Miles tried to look like he knew that already, though if he'd ever been over this route, I figured he'd be lecturing me on it. "We got a box in the baggage car ahead ridin' on our tickets," he told the conductor who said it would be shifted at Carbondale and not to worry about it.

Uncle Miles replied, "I will worry about it as long as it's my responsibility. There's a feller back in the parlor car—a big red-necked rebel, very mouthy, who will steal that box if he has half a chance."

The conductor found that somewhat humorous. He looked Uncle Miles over, noting he wore an old blue suit under a pair of overalls, which was his complete traveling outfit. "So you reckon to be robbed by a parlor-car passenger. What are you shipping, a trunk full of gold-mine shares?"

"No," said Uncle Miles, squinting at him, "a dead body." The conductor moved on.

A candy butcher came through next, selling oddments off a tray. "Never buy eats on a train, Alexander," Uncle Miles said. "They charge two prices. I had some sandwiches made up which will see us through." He patted his tool kit that doubled as a valise. "I reckon your dad give you money, but it isn't for throwin' around."

It was nearly dark when we pulled in at Carbondale. "We're gettin' into foreign parts now," he said. "They call this end of the state Little Egypt, and they'd as soon cut your throat as to look at you. It's rough territory."

The *Panama Limited* was waiting for our train, and quite a number of passengers crossed the platform to get on it. I recognized Brulatour by his white suit, skipping across from one parlor car to another. The box with Inez was already on a baggage cart, and Uncle Miles watched until it was put aboard. He told me to skin on up into the train and stake out a pair of facing seats. And that was how I happened to be looking out the window in time to see a surprising sight.

Just as the platform cleared of passengers, somebody jumped down out of the baggage car of the Bluff City train and rocketed across to the *Panama Limited*. In the dimness I saw it was Blossom Culp, swinging a bundle of her possessions tied up in a bandanna.

Then the platform was empty but for the trunk handlers who were rolling the carts away. And I knew Blossom had transferred to the New Orleans train the same as we had, only quicker. I'd told her already that she's everywhere at once, and she seemed bent on proving the point.

When I woke up next morning, palm trees were flashing past the train window, like the fluttering pages of a Sunday school paper. I'd slept with my feet out in the aisle and had sweated through my knicker suit. Uncle Miles was sitting up, very alert, but his teeth were out. "State of Mississippi," he managed to say, "stinkin' hot and dirt poor." The plush on the seat prickled something fierce, and with a sandwich in my pocket I set off to the washroom. When I was done in there, I kept walking through the train.

I stumbled along through four coaches and the dining car, and nobody stopped me. There were caged-off parts to the baggage car, but not locked up. I counted four coffins among the jumble of trunks before I finally spied the bronze handles on Inez's box. And unless I'd been having one of my visions back on the Carbondale platform, I figured Blossom was not far off in this traveling graveyard.

"All right," I yelled out over the train noise. "Rear up, Blossom! I know you're in here."

And above a pile of swaying crates Blossom's head

rose. Her hair was a bird's nest, and planted on top was a sad old straw hat. She appeared to have passed a sleepless night. I gave her the kind of out-of-patience look that Uncle Miles often gave people.

And she said, "I can go where I please. I got twenty-eight dollars of my own money."

"I don't doubt that," I told her. "You got it selling trips through our barn. And what'll your mama think when you turn up missing?"

"She don't care," Blossom said. "It's just one less mouth to feed to her."

"How come you're stowing away among the coffins and the baggage if you're so flush with money?"

"I was afraid they wouldn't sell me a ticket, and I didn't know what it might cost. Besides, I'm guarding this box here. I'm going to help you see Inez safely to her rest."

"Many thanks for that," I sneered, "but I guess Uncle Miles and I can handle those arrangements."

"Maybe you can," she replied, "but all I know is that the Brulatour fellow was nosing around this baggage car late last night, and where was you then? He'll steal your thunder if he can and Inez too."

"Blossom, you're the champion busybody of the world. I don't see where you fit into things at all."

"You have the Gift and could see Inez's spirit with your own eyes and hear her words too. I ain't receptive, but I got some wisdom you don't. I know what it's like to be lonesome, like she was." She turned her face away. Though her chin looked firm, her mouth quivered. And I saw that I had maybe said the wrong thing.

"Well then, as long as you're here, you better come back to the chair car with me and Uncle Miles."

"And get flung off the train by the conductor for not paying? No, indeed." Blossom shut her eyes and shook her head.

"Oh come on, Blossom, like as not he won't even notice you."

"Some people can see me clearer than you can, Alexander. You can see a dead girl easier than a living one. But I reckon you will change in time."

"That's a silly thing to say, Blossom," I told her, but in a way I knew it wasn't. "They'll only catch you when we pull into New Orleans."

"They didn't catch me at Carbondale," she replied, and her head sank below the packing cases. I handed the sandwich down to her, which she took.

Heading back through the train, I was determined to tell Uncle Miles that Blossom was a stowaway. But I lost my resolve since nothing much could be done about her short of New Orleans anyhow.

He thought I'd been absent longer than necessary, so I got him talking to take his mind off that. "What are we going to do when we get down there?"

"Do? Well, first and last we're goin' to keep that Brulatour feller from makin' a public spectacle and hoggin' the attention. And we're goin' to put up at a quiet place that takes payin' guests and then scout around to find the graveyard where the Dumaine folks is laid away. Then we're goin' to stick Inez in with them. And of course I will be showin' you somethin' of the city."

"How are you going to do that, Uncle Miles, in a place you've never been before?"

"Why, boy, I been to New Orleans! There and back on a riverboat. I been everywhere I ever wanted to go and two or three places I never even wanted to see! I have lived a long time, Alexander, and most of it with itchy feet."

"Oh," I said.

"I was down to New Orleans in—lemme see—eighteen hundred and ninety-one. It was the time the Black Hand murdered the police chief, and then they was all lynched in Congo Square. The Black Hand is a gang of outlaws and like as not they still flourish, as anything evil will down there.

"Oh, there is lessons to be learned in New Orleans you won't find in your school books, Alexander. It is a town entirely give over to fleshly pleasure, a free and easy place, full of people walkin' abroad who anywhere else would be in jail or a madhouse. High livin' and low livin', good drink and bad women . . ."

Uncle Miles shook his head and seemed to go off into a reverie. "Music day and night," he mumbled. "The cars clatterin' and the women callin' from the balconies, and the boats hootin' over the levee. I guess it's about as fine a place as I know of." Then he nodded off to sleep and didn't stir till we were under the canopy of the New Orleans depot.

People move different down in New Orleans. That was the first thing I noticed about the place, before we were even off the train. They bounce and sashay along like they're in a musical play on the stage. There was a brass band playing on the platform, and the bandsmen shuffled their feet in time to their song. They were playing "Nearer My God to Thee" in ragtime.

When Uncle Miles heard the music, he was on his feet, squinting out the open window. "That's one of them burial society bands!" he said, banging his fist on the window. "And looky over there past them gates. They got a horse-drawn hearse backed up. Look at them purple plumes on them horses!

"Well, Alexander, that big-mouth Brulatour and his newspaper has got us outflanked. He'll turn the whole thing into a vaudeville act.

"I was in hopes we'd be left to go about our business in peace, but they're too many for us. Seemed like we was the only family Inez had, Yankees though we are, and not even Catholics. I took it as a sign when she appeared to you, since I've felt bad carryin' the old captain's guilty secret these many years. I wanted to do right by her before my time was up."

The train had come to a halt by then, and people were crowding down the aisle. But Uncle Miles sat in his seat, and I'd never seen him look as whipped. Frail even. I cast about for something to perk his spirit. But all I could think of was that Blossom in the baggage car was the only ace in the hole we had and hardly worth mentioning.

Brulatour's big straw hat bobbed past the window, and he was shortly to be seen surrounded by his newspaper brethren. There were some ladies crowding around him too, in big hats with parasols or fans. He was bowing and scraping to them. In New Orleans they put their socializing before business.

Which is not Blossom's way.

❧ 20 ❧

"KEEP A-WALKIN' AND DON'T GET drawed into that Brulatour mob," Uncle Miles said when we got off the train. But nobody marked us as we dragged our valises toward the gates.

I had my eye out for Blossom and saw her right away up by the baggage car. She was on the platform, holding the bandanna full of her traveling gear behind her. She seemed to be passing the time of day with the men who were unloading the train. I never saw her look any more innocent.

Farther off, I noticed one of the big coffins from the train being eased into the fancy hearse. And that offered something heartening to say to Uncle Miles. "If that hearse is for Inez, they have got into a mix-up over the boxes."

"Oh there is my brother now who I have come down to the station to meet," Blossom sang out and pointed a finger at me. "And that fancy box with the handles up in the baggage car belongs to him!"

"Things is happenin' pretty fast," Uncle Miles muttered to me. "Who is that peculiar-lookin' little gal?"

I told him she was one of us, since there was no time to go into detail. Then I peered over my shoulder to see if Brulatour was bearing down on us. But he was still in the knot of his confederates and admirers.

Between us, Blossom and I could just heft the box. "Cut out," Uncle Miles said. "I am just behind you." And I guess Brulatour was so sure of his triumph that he didn't check his hearse, for we saw it clopping away as we climbed up into a jitney. Our driver strapped Inez's box on the back.

Uncle Miles asked him if he knew where St. Charles Avenue was. The driver told him it was hard to miss as it was the major boulevard of the city. "Then see if you can find Mrs. Pomarade's Colonnade Guest House on it, for that's where we're puttin' up." The driver replied that Mrs. Pomarade was as hard to miss as the boulevard. And then we drove off through the steamy brick streets of New Orleans.

Blossom had no more experience riding in jitneys than I had. But she straightened her hat, crossed her ankles in her high-topped shoes, and put on quite a ladylike display.

"I don't believe I've had the pleasure," Uncle Miles said, peering past me at her.

"This here is Blossom Culp," I said. "She stowed away in the baggage car and is from Bluff City."

"A Bluff City girl and I don't know her?" said Uncle Miles, very puzzled.

"My people are not in a position to have much carpentry done," she told him, very dignified. There was a show of understanding between them from the first minute, and I felt somewhat left out.

"I take it you have run off," he said, "which is liable to be a worry to your folks."

"Very little worries them," she replied, "and roving is in our blood."

"Now that," Uncle Miles said firmly, "is a thing I can understand. It appears you worked a switch with a couple of bodies. That bein' the case, how'd you do it?"

Blossom held up her bandanna bundle. "I had a pencil stub in this poke," she said. "And last night I come across a shipping label on the floor of the baggage car. One of them that says This End Up. It was a blank one, and it come to me I might put it to use. So I lettered on it Body of Inez Dumaine, New Orleans. My spelling is good, and my lettering is even better." Blossom folded her hands primly in her lap.

"Yes, go on," Uncle Miles urged her.

"Well, I had me a look around at some of the other coffins being shipped south and tried to figure which they'd unload first. I picked one, peeled the label off it, and stuck my new one on. It wasn't a sure thing, but it worked."

"Well damn me to hell," said Uncle Miles, staring at her in deep admiration.

"So when we pulled into New Orleans this evening, I nipped out of the baggage car and through the car where they eat and eased down out of the train when nobody noticed. Then I stepped up to where you seen me on the platform. There wasn't nothin' to it."

"Alexander," Uncle Miles jabbed me hard in the ribs. "There sets a girl with all her wits about her."

I said nothing.

Mrs. Pomarade's Colonnade Guest House, while needing paint, was an immense fine place with a leading glass front door behind pillars. There was only a small sign in the yard to tell it was a private hotel. A maid answered. She took a long look at the three of us and nearly shut the door. But Uncle Miles boomed, "Tell her Miles Armsworth from up yonder."

We all pushed the box into the front hall. The maid didn't like that, and later when she learned what it contained, she took fright. We were shown into a sitting room being dusted by another maid. She worked her feather duster and her hips together in a snappy rhythm. And she was singing at the top of her voice, "If you ain't gonna shake it, what'd you bring it for?"

Presently, a very unusual-looking big woman stepped in from the hall. I'd never seen anything to equal her appearance, and haven't since. Her face was made up very clownish, and there were brush strokes painted above her eyes to represent lashes. She wore a large and lacey dress, mostly yellow, and high-heeled shoes with no backs to them. There was a variety of combs in her hair, which must have been the reddest in America.

"Why Miles Armsworth!" she said, "Aren't you dead? The girl said you was from up yonder, but now I see she only meant Bluff City. It's grand to see you, you old b—"

"Sophie," Uncle Miles interrupted, "can you put us up?"

"I can put you up, but can I put up with you? That's the question." She laughed immoderately at her joke. "Who are these young'uns? You don't mean to tell me that at your time of life you—"

"This here is my great-nephew, Alexander. Say how do you do to Mrs. Pomarade, Alexander. And this here is Miss Blossom Culp, who is—ah—travelin' with us."

"My stars," said Mrs. Pomarade, "quite a party!"

"There's one more to our party," Uncle Miles said. "Out in your hall is a box with Inez Dumaine in it."

Mrs. Pomarade looked behind her in some surprise. "Not *the* Inez Dumaine I been reading about in the *Delta Daily?* The poor thing who—"

"The same," said Uncle Miles.

"That's not a very big box, considering, is it?" Mrs. Pomarade said.

"In fifty years' time you won't make quite such a big package yourself, Sophie," remarked Uncle Miles.

Mrs. Pomarade showed Uncle Miles and me up to a room. Then she took Blossom off with her. These two must have confided in one another off on their own, for Mrs. Pomarade thereafter seemed to know all about our business. When we were alone, I said to Uncle Miles, "Was that Mrs. Pomarade an actress at one time?"

"Very likely. She's had a busy life," is all he said.

We washed up and he peeled off his overalls. Then he was ready to go down to dinner in his blue suit. He told me to change into a clean shirt, which coming from him was something of a surprise.

We cooled our heels downstairs in the sitting room long after the dinner gong went. A few other guests shuffled into the dining room, but there was still no sign of Mrs. Pomarade or Blossom.

"Nobody's ever in a hurry down here," Uncle Miles observed. "Time don't mean nothin' to them."

My belly was flapping against my backbone from starvation when a young lady entered the room. Not wishing to stare, I examined her feet. They were small and neat, shod in a pair of little high-heeled shoes with bows. Above the bows were a pair of ankles in lace stockings. And above that a pink and white skirt held up by a small hand. Here is a dainty dish, I thought, feeling quite worldly. Then I looked up into the face of Blossom Culp.

She'd been transformed by Mrs. Pomarade, and no wonder it took so long. The dress came near to fitting Blossom, though it was filled out in the busts. Her hair was scooped up off her neck. She looked fifteen at the youngest, and her lips were rouged.

I was on my feet, suffering shock. "Evenin', Blossom," Uncle Miles said, though how he knew her I don't understand.

Mrs. Pomarade stepped up behind her creation, beaming. She had put on a different dress herself, which was black and busy. So I took it that dressing up for dinner in New Orleans was an ordinary thing you weren't to remark on.

"I trust you have kept your same good appetite, Miles," she said.

"Sophie, I am in all respects the same man you knowed better'n twenty years ago."

"Better'n twenty years! Don't tell me it's been that long!"

"Oh, you was nothin' but a young girl at the time," said Uncle Miles.

"That's stretching a point somewhat. But then you always were a smooth-talking devil, Miles. Let's step in to dinner." She took his arm and I had no recourse but to offer Blossom mine.

Since she was altered out of all recognition, I whispered at her, "Blossom, if you aren't a sow's ear turned into a silk purse!"

"You always were a smooth-talking devil, Alexander," she replied, smiling straight ahead at the dining room.

Having watched Mrs. Van Deeter drink coffee, I thought I'd seen elegant manners, but Blossom surpassed all. There was crabmeat to begin with, and her hand shot out for the smallest fork. There was gumbo soup, and her hand went directly to a spoon with a round bowl. There was a shrimp sauce that the maid poured over rice, and Blossom leaned back to be served. And at the end, there were bowls of water for washing up. In them were sprigs of mint and lemon slices. Blossom flicked this floating stuff aside and dipped her fingertips in the water.

She ate everything in sight, but you never saw anything so grand. Then I saw her black eyes were on Mrs. Pomarade the whole time. And she was copying her at every point with very close timing.

Uncle Miles was deep in conversation regarding our mission. His eyes were pink and watery, but his spectacles flashed. "Sophie, if it is all the same to you, I'd as soon leave that box of bones in your front hall as to let it fall into Brulatour's hands. I want Inez settled, but that feller has got my dander up, and I'll rob him of his newspaper story if I can."

Mrs. Pomarade nodded, mentioning that as secrecy would work to our advantage, he'd better keep his voice down. "Those young'uns there are quiet enough," she observed. "Are they sweethearts?"

"Certainly not," said Blossom, patting her upswept back hair just like Lucille does.

"Let's us stick to business," said Uncle Miles. "How are we goin' to locate the Dumaines' cemetery plot? If memory serves me, this entire town's half graveyard."

"Oh Miles," said Mrs. Pomarade, "the everlasting *Delta Daily* has been crowing over this business for days. Everybody in the city knows by now that the Dumaines are all in the old Cemetery Number One over on Basin Street.

"Why there was even a photograph of the family tomb in yesterday's paper. Though how Mortimer Brulatour will explain to his readers the wrong body I don't know." She wheezed considerably with laughter, and some of the pencil marks above her eyes melted and ran down the seams in her face. "I do hope we can escape his notice when we take Inez to her crypt, for he'll be shamed and looking for satisfaction. And now I don't see why we can't excuse these young'uns to the parlor while we have a drop of brandy and recollect old times."

When we were off to ourselves, Blossom unbended somewhat from her new appearance, though she was still so vastly changed that it put me on edge.

We had the parlor to ourselves as all the rest of the hotel guests had made for the porch rockers. Though there were plenty of chairs, we sat together on a sofa. Blossom kicked her feet forward to examine the bows on her little high-heeled shoes.

"Well, Blossom," I said in a voice that was cracking again, "Bluff City wouldn't recognize you now."

"It never did, Alexander," she answered.

Not knowing what to say to that, I fiddled with the tassels on the antimacassar. Finally I said, "Maybe Mrs.

166

Pomarade would let you take those clothes home with you."

"If she did, her maid wouldn't have nothing to wear on her evenings off. Besides, where would I go tricked up like this? Do you reckon Lucille would invite me up on your porch to drink tea?" She grinned bitterly at this.

"You always think Lucille is a humorous topic," I said. "But I can tell you otherwise. She liked to tear me limb from limb just the other night. And I'll tell you something else," I said, leaning over toward the pearl in her ear. "It's my opinion that she has switched over from Tom Hackett to Lowell Seaforth. And though Lowell is an intelligent fellow, I suspect he's fallen for her."

Blossom shook her head and closed her eyes in the old way. "Oh, Alexander, you are a true dunce in matters of love. There's no need to suspect what's clear as day. Lowell and Lucille are just as taken with each other as —Uncle Miles and Mrs. Pomarade."

"Uncle Miles?" I said, scandalized. "Why he's too independent and too old. You are a peculiar girl with peculiar notions, Blossom, but I thought you had better sense."

"Come on," she sighed, slipping off the sofa. She stood up and put out her hand. "Follow me and tread lightly."

We crept out into the shadows of the hallway and peered through a potted palm tree. There was only one light left on in the dining room, and under it Uncle Miles and Mrs. Pomarade still sat at the table.

Their brandy glasses touched, and their heads were close. He was murmuring some tale, and Mrs. Pomarade's head was nodding in time to it. In the dim pink light you couldn't see that they were old. They might have been anybody. They might have been me and Blossom Culp.

❦ 21 ❧

UNCLE MILES WAS ALREADY OUT OF HIS
bed and gone when I stirred next morning. I couldn't
place where I was at first, what with the palm trees outside throwing their greenish color into the room.

When I got down to the parlor, Mrs. Pomarade was
reading aloud from a newspaper to an audience of Blossom and Uncle Miles. The *Delta Daily* had dropped
their commentary on Inez altogether. But their rival, the
Louisiana Ledger, evidently had a spy in the enemy
ranks. Mrs. Pomarade was quoting from the latter:

Our worthy competitors at the Delta Daily *have
suffered a setback in promoting the myth of the
Ghost Girl. The long-lost daughter of a once-
prominent local family was to be returned from
her northern "grave" on last evening's Panama
Limited.*

The hoax was revealed in a strictly private

Delta Daily *conference when Mortimer Brulatour of the* Delta *staff introduced a mislabeled coffin to his colleagues. An examination of the contents revealed an unidentified, recently deceased male in good condition, origins and destination unknown. Mortimer Brulatour has not made himself available for comment.*

Thus ends another attempt by the desperate Delta Daily *to add readers, by fair means or foul, to their declining subscription list. Anyone expecting the body of a recently deceased male in good condition wearing a pinstriped suit and a Knights of Columbus lodge ring is urged to contact the* Delta *editorial staff who are not above preying upon the unsuspecting and bereaved in their relentless pursuit of yellow journalism.*

Mrs. Pomarade ceased reading and wiped daintily at her eyes. "I know it's a confounded outrage, but I can't help but see the humor in it." She cast a foxy look at Blossom, who only stared deeply into her coffee cup and looked smug.

Two of the hotel gardeners came into the front hall and bore Inez's box away. The four of us issued quickly out behind it. On the side drive an old plug was hitched up to a buckboard. The gardeners spread a rug to conceal the box once it was on the wagon bed.

Then, with some puffing, Mrs. Pomarade and Uncle Miles climbed on the seat, and Blossom and I edged up on the tailgate and let our feet dangle. No onlooker would have known what we were about. There was something of the traveling patent-medicine show about us.

Uncle Miles squinted like an Indian in the sunlight and had turned his workshirt sleeves well back. In the open air, Mrs. Pomarade's hair was fierier than ever nature intended, though she subdued it somewhat with a motoring veil and a parasol. Blossom wore her own shoes, which were more practical for a graveyard. But she had on another of the maid's outfits. What with that and a sunshade she held in imitation of Mrs. Pomarade, she maintained some of her new grandeur.

I took it we were avoiding the main boulevards as much as we could. We threaded through streets where people were doing a big fruit and vegetable business on the curb. There were dark archways behind where others drank coffee and hard liquor under ceiling fans. It was a picturesque trip but long. And we stole along like thieves on an outing.

We were an hour getting to the Cemetery Number One on Basin Street. Though I had dreamed about a New Orleans graveyard, the place came as a surprise. There was marble in plenty above ground, but all in a ruinous state. It was more like an ancient city, much plundered, than I had bargained for. At the gate, Mrs. Pomarade handed down money to the caretaker to point out our way and to seal his lips.

The tombs were laid out along gravel streets. Most of

them were overgrown, with here and there an urn of dried-up flowers. The sun pounded down, and occasionally a snake's tail flipped off hot marble and into a cool crevice. It was as weird as any daylit spot could well be. Blossom peered out from under her sunshade at the wonder of it, but kept silent.

Some of the statuary, though chipped, was quite interesting. And I wouldn't have minded the place except that the individual crypts were stacked up like dresser drawers, and several had been stove in, revealing crumbling interiors. Before we got where we were going, I was downright homesick for the idea of burying people six feet down under a low mound.

Presently we drew up to a big family tomb as tall as an outhouse and several times longer. It was in an advanced state of decay, but the name Dumaine was still clear in carved letters at the top. There were maybe twenty or so places for bodies. Some of the cubbyholes were covered by square marble fronts with French names on them, mossed over. Others were open to the air, and the fragments of their fronts littered the ground. All the Dumaines seemed to have done their dying a good while back. There was a little lawn before the tomb, surrounded by a cast-iron fence with an open gate. We'd come at last to the place Inez's restless spirit had hankered over down through the years.

I helped Mrs. Pomarade down from the wagon in stages. Uncle Miles was already reaching for the box, but she murmured, "Let the young'uns do it, Miles." Blossom and I stepped up to pull it out ourselves. The box wouldn't fit into any of the open spaces, and we all stood quiet under the blazing sun. It was a likely time for devotions, but none of us were praying-aloud people.

At length, Uncle Miles said, "Sophie, why don't you take these children on a walk while I do what needs doing."

Then I knew what had to be done, but I listened to Mrs. Pomarade explaining. "Cemeteries are crowded places down here, so it's our way to use the same space over and over. As a rule, when a body's been in one of these tombs a few years, it's taken out, the coffin opened, and the bones disposed of. Then the space is used again. Well, these Dumaines have plenty of room, and I reckon under the unusual circumstances we'd better put Inez's bones in one of these open spaces."

She looked at Blossom and me from under her parasol, and in that dimness her face looked less clownish and more kind. "I think that would satisfy Inez, don't you?"

When Blossom and I nodded, she said, "And so let's take a stroll around the grounds. I'll give you a look at the tomb of Marie Laveau, the Voodoo Queen, which is a spot all the tourists visit."

Blossom's hand stole over and clutched mine, and I knew she meant to hold her ground. We neither of us had come all this way to be led around like children.

"No, ma'am," I said, "We'd like to see the Voodoo Queen's place, but not till later. I—we'll help Uncle Miles put Inez's bones in. It's only right."

"Let them," she said to Uncle Miles. He handed over a claw hammer from out of the buckboard, and I dropped down to pry up the box lid.

I worked all around it until the nails were standing high, and I remembered Uncle Miles's old story about the man buried alive. My breath was coming in short gasps and sweat ran down my face. And when the last nail was lifted, I sat back on my heels. Uncle Miles reached down and took both sides of the lid in his thorny hands and lifted it clear.

I looked aside to see Mrs. Pomarade cross herself in a slow, private way. Blossom skitted off to one side and seemed to disappear. Uncle Miles reached in first and took out a human skull. He stretched past me and thrust it way back into the cavity of the tomb, first peering into the darkness in case a snake might be in there. The sun danced around in the open box—white bones against white, satiny stuff. It was more like a coffin within than without, and I didn't care for it.

I reached for the little skull—Trixie's, or whatever her real name had been. It was as warm as life and rested in the hollow of my hand. I remembered the draggled little bit of pink ribbon and the damp tangles in the fur. You won't need to whimper any more, Trixie, I said, but not aloud.

We worked faster then and got caught up in the

rhythm of the job. I reached without looking and pushed bones of various sizes into the cool place. In a moment the box was empty except for some crumbs of dirt from our backyard which I flung out on the hard-baked New Orleans ground.

"She's home now," Mrs. Pomarade said, "bless her heart." Uncle Miles stood up and wiped the sweat off his brow. I stayed crouched where I was, and when I looked one last time into the box, my eyes swam.

Uncle Miles's hand dropped on my shoulder. From far overhead he said, "Old folks don't grieve over the mystery of death. But Alexander, you ain't old."

There was no sign that Inez knew she was home, and the white bones were a far cry from the heart-shaped face and rustling skirts in our barn. There wasn't any sign of contentment from inside the peculiar tomb. Nor any moan of welcome from Inez's people, whose own bones had maybe been cleared out who knows when. Inez was gone from me for good. And I was setting forth into life at just the age she'd left it, and doors seemed to clang shut through all the years between us. It was a fanciful thought, I know, and I didn't in fact hear doors clanging. But I knew a time had passed that wouldn't come again. And I knew as sure as if Blossom's mama had said so that I no longer had the Gift and that there'd be no place for being receptive to the Spirit World in my future.

Then Blossom darted out from behind the tomb, busy as ever. Her finery was wilted, and her hair was frizzing out of control. As a result, she looked her normal self. In her hands was a double bunch of tired flowers clearly filched from other graves. She stepped up to Inez's shelf and jammed the bouquet in as far as it would go. One black-red gladiolus drooped down outside.

Nobody pointed out to her that she'd robbed the dead to honor the dead. But still, she turned and said, "It was all I could think of to do."

"It was right," said Mrs. Pomarade.

I hammered the lid back on Inez's box, and Blossom and I slid it back on the wagon. Then we all made off, but took the long way around to see the tomb of Marie Laveau, the Voodoo Queen, who was well known in New Orleans circles.

According to Mrs. Pomarade, Marie dealt in strong potions and various charms and generally had quite a hold on people down there during her lifetime. People still visited her tomb. There were X's scrawled all over it in brick dust, which is considered lucky. The grass before it was all worn bald, and that's part of the ritual too. People wishing to be on the safe side of her spirit mark up her tomb and then shuffle their feet at her door.

Mrs. Pomarade wanted to know if we cared to pay our respects, but neither Blossom nor I did. I for one was done with all that and ready for the living world.

With no reason for stealth, Uncle Miles aimed the horse into the heart of town. We passed along through the old quarter where the cast-iron porches hang well out to shade the pavement. We'd likely not have turned into the main drag, Royal Street, except that the buckboard wheels wedged with a curving trolley track, and we were in the thick of the traffic before we knew it.

Royal Street is given over chiefly to banks and fine shops, though much of it is the worse for wear. Women balancing laundry bundles on their heads mingled with top-hatted bankers. The smell of brewing coffee blended with horse-droppings, and there was nothing of the graveyard to this part of the city.

We were just drawing along past the new Monteleone Hotel when we heard shouts. Since Blossom and I were facing backwards off the end of the wagon bed, we weren't the first to take notice. But when the horse stopped and reared up, I was on my feet. Hanging onto the bridle up front was Mortimer Brulatour, howling his head off.

Mrs. Pomarade quivered some but held her ground, and Uncle Miles was on his feet, grabbing for a buggy whip that wasn't there.

"Scroundrels!" Brulatour bawled. His face was purple, and his big white hat rolled into the gutter. "Yankee trash!" he shrieked, alarming the horse dangerously. "Mortimer Brulatour does not play the fool to a bunch of—"

From there, his fulminations seemed to lead him into another language, French possibly. Apparently we weren't far from the *Delta Daily* offices as several of his ink-stained minions stepped cautiously out of the gathering crowd.

"It's a hot day to get too worked up," Uncle Miles said from his lofty perch. Loud as Uncle Miles often was, he sounded quite calm compared to Brulatour. "State your business, man, and watch your language. There is ladies present."

"Ladies!" wailed Brulatour, at the end of his rope. "Listen, you dried-up old rube, you have all but cost me my job by stealing the body of Inez Dumaine! If you think a tin-horn old ghoul and a couple of brats are going to rob me of my good name—"

More French. But Mortimer Brulatour gestured to his flunkies to grab Inez's box out of the wagon. I was ready to make a stand, and no doubt Blossom was prepared to light into them with the claw hammer. But Uncle Miles turned to look right at me and winked once behind his spectacles. "Well, they have us outnumbered, Alexander," he said in quite a loud voice. "Better give them what they are after."

I was so caught up in the events, I'd forgotten the box was empty. When Brulatour's henchmen reached up into the wagon bed, I obliged them by scooting the box their way. As it slid past her, Blossom pointed to the top of it and said to them, "This end up."

"Well, I reckon this will restore your rightful name!" Uncle Miles called out after Brulatour. But he was shooing his men with the box through the crowd and didn't favor us with a backward look. "And," said Uncle Miles in a voice just for us, "I reckon he figured we were goin' *to* the cemetery, not *from.*"

✺ 22 ✺

THAT LAST EVENING IN NEW ORLEANS, Mrs. Pomarade brought out a bottle of Madeira wine before supper. Blossom and I were allowed a half measure apiece. I gulped mine, and it went straight to my head. But this was Blossom's last time to be elegant, and she sipped hers with her little finger stuck out very refined. She wouldn't have said no to a refill.

Mrs. Pomarade brought out an extra glass to represent Inez, and we all toasted her. I can still see the way the pink light from the chandelier broke into red rainbows when it hit the wine. Then Uncle Miles threw Inez's glass into the grate, and we raised ours to her one more time.

The maid started in with our supper plates, and Blossom reached for her napkin. Something rolled out of its folds and wobbled across the tablecloth. Her hand was after it like lightning striking. Then she held it up, and it was Inez's brooch, the one with the human-hair flowers.

Her eyes got rounder and darker, if possible, and she looked at Uncle Miles. He blinked back at her from behind his spectacles. "Is it for me?" she whispered.

"I have an idee it must be," he replied, and Blossom fixed it among the ruffles on her chest. She was never without it somewhere on her person from that evening on.

Later that night when we were off to ourselves, I told Uncle Miles he'd been pretty cute to hide the brooch that way in Blossom's napkin. "Alexander," he said, "I mislaid that brooch on the very day we opened the grave back home. I ain't seen it again until this evenin', and it comes as quite an astonishment to me. And I am too old to be astonished by much."

"Aw, Uncle Miles," I said, wanting to be skeptical.

"Boy, I don't lie." And I guess that after a lifetime of truth-telling he didn't. Maybe it truly was the last time that Inez Dumaine worked in our lives.

That night I lay abed sleepless long after Uncle Miles commenced a steady snoring. Outside, the St. Charles Avenue trolleys rattled by, reminding me of home. And when I slept, I dreamed I was dancing between the streetcar rails in my nightshirt. But I wasn't alone. Blossom was dancing with me, in hers.

Mrs. Pomarade saw us off down at the New Orleans depot. When it came time to board, she clasped hands with Uncle Miles and looked long at him from under her hat brim. I turned away from a couple of oldsters occupying themselves in this way. But I heard her say, "Come again, Miles, you old reprobate. You will never be a stranger here with Sophie."

And he replied, "Let's us speak plain, Sophie. My travelin' days is drawin' to an end, but I will carry you in my heart." According to Blossom's account later, they kissed then. But when I looked up, Uncle Miles was digging his tobacco tin out of his overall bib, and someone down the platform was calling the train.

We found a pair of facing seats, but Uncle Miles stood at the window until the train moved, looking out at the platform. Mrs. Pomarade put up her hand at the last moment and then turned and walked away, less lively than she had been.

For this journey Blossom rode in the chair car as Uncle Miles's guest. To my certain knowledge, she never spent a penny of that ill-gotten twenty-eight dollars and very likely still has it.

I slept a good part of the way, and so did Blossom. She sat next to Uncle Miles with her frizzy head wedged up against his arm and Inez's brooch hanging off her middy collar and her spider legs curled up under her. She was a sorry-looking sight again. But she had grit and possibilities, and I knew I'd have my work cut out for me just keeping up with her in the future.

I remember the three of us just that way, rolling along north through the hot afternoon, heading home. Blossom and I in a stupor from our adventures and the wine. And Uncle Miles awake and alert, with a far-off look in his eyes and Mrs. Pomarade in his heart.

Not many months after that, Uncle Miles passed away. All of Bluff City turned out for his funeral, and Mrs. Van Deeter herself carried a big wreath of roses up to the side of the grave.

By then, Lowell and Lucille were engaged, and Mother was busy by day and night with the wedding arrangements. The invitations were ordered engraved from a St. Louis firm, and Cousin Elvera was scheduled to pour. But these events don't bear on my story, for by then very few people even remembered that I'd once seen a ghost in the brick barn out in the back of our place.